HILLBILLY VAMP

R.E. Holding

CLIFF CAVE
BOOKS, LLC

Cliff Cave Books, LLC

For information contact :

http://www.cliffcavebooks.com

Cover art by Get Covers

Cover design by R.E. Holding

Interior design by R.E. Holding

ISBN (paperback): 978-1-963125-08-5

ISBN (paperback): 979-8-224-49893-2

ISBN (paperback): 978-1-963125-15-3

ISBN (ebook): 978-1-963125-09-2

ISBN (audiobook): 978-1-963125-14-6

First Edition: 2024

10 9 8 7 6 5 4 3 2 1

CONTENTS

1

THE MINE

GOING ON PATROL NEAR the town border may have been a little out of their jurisdiction.

"What were the complaints again?" Wyatt scratched his nose as he and the sheriff moved through rotting forest debris.

"There've been suspicious sightings of someone roaming around the woods," the sheriff said.

Wyatt was unsatisfied. Why were they out so far beyond their usual patrol?

"I know that look in your eye," the sheriff said. "We're out here because we need to comb the whole area just in case."

"Couldn't we have asked for help from Mulberry's sheriff and crew? I mean, I'm getting tired."

The sheriff chuffed. "They're already taking care of the other side. Don't worry—it won't be much longer."

"But if we don't find anything *now*, there's going to be a tomorrow..." Wyatt sighed and slumped his shoulders. He'd never wanted to be a deputy in the small town of Royal Lake. He'd merely taken the position when his best friend from grade school had become sheriff. "Birdseed," they called him. To this day, he didn't know why.

"Shh! What was that?" Birdseed froze on the spot. Wyatt turned to stone.

An eerie silence penetrated the forest. The only sound was the faint breeze cutting through tree branches. Birdseed hovered his hand over the pistol on his hip.

As they stood silent and still, a distant rustle shook the brush. Both men turned toward the noise. After a moment, Birdseed relaxed and circled around, pulling a pack of cigarettes from his pants pocket.

"Probably a raccoon," he said, tapping a stick from the pack and squeezing it in the corner of his mouth.

"You think?" Wyatt rubbed his face, tracing his mouth like a goatee.

"Nope." He blew out a puff of smoke.

Wyatt waved the air in front of him. "Those'll kill you."

"So will fast food." Birdseed nodded at Wyatt's belly.

"Hey, food sustains life! I can't help that I like food."

"Yeah, sure."

The brush rustled in the distance. "There it is again," Wyatt whispered.

Their radios simultaneously crackled, causing Birdseed to jump and fumble around for the volume knob. Wyatt flipped his radio off.

Another rustle. There was something in the distance. It stood there, stiff as a board, staring in their direction. Wyatt saw the reflection in its eyes, making it look like a wild animal.

"That's no raccoon," Wyatt whispered.

Birdseed ducked down and slid his taser from its holster. He wiped his brow, staring back at the thing and spitting out his cigarette. It smoked in the wet grass. Slowly, he stuck out a leg to stub it out.

Sweat rolled down Wyatt's temple, and time slowed down as they tried to make sense of what they saw in front of them.

"What do we do?" Wyatt hissed.

Birdseed lifted his taser and opened his mouth to shout at it. Before he could make a sound, the figure darted to the side, out of sight.

Wyatt perked up. "What the...?"

"Let's go," Birdseed said. He swung around Wyatt and jogged in the direction of the stranger.

Wyatt wasn't entirely sure they had seen anything. It was probably a mountain lion, and they were chasing their own doom. He panted as he ran after his friend.

He thought he saw the blur of a grayish-white flash through the trees. The hairs on his arms prickled as the form disappeared again. He smacked into Birdseed's back after he stopped in his tracks.

"Damn, dude! Watch yourself." Birdseed pulled out another cigarette and clamped it between his teeth.

"Why'd you stop?"

Birdseed shrugged. "We're getting close to our border. If that thing went across it, it's Mulberry's problem."

"Oh. Well, I..."

"Hey, do you see that over there?"

Birdseed pointed a tar-yellowed finger north in the direction of his newfound attention. Wyatt tried to peer around a nearby thick swath of trees. After a little effort see-sawing his neck, he caught it: a tiny pinprick of light in the distance.

"You ever see a light over there before?" he asked.

"I've never been out this far before, so no."

"Do you think the thing went that way?"

Wyatt didn't care. He wasn't interested in pursuing this ghost; it gave him the creeps. He shrugged.

"Let's go check it out," said Birdseed.

It wasn't a question—it was a demand. Rolling his eyes, Wyatt trudged behind his friend. He was already worn out from the first jog. However, he wondered if Birdseed was right about his weight. His chest felt tight, and his trousers felt tighter. He jammed his thumbs under the waistband to adjust them over his gut.

"I wonder if there's a cabin out here." Birdseed turned with that cursed cigarette still poking out from his lip. How he could breathe was anyone's guess.

"I don't know about any cabin," Wyatt huffed as his feet dragged, "but if we do find one, I don't know if I want to stick around to find out who owns it."

"Don't be yellow. I mean, we've got all kinds of weapons." He stopped to let Wyatt catch up, then flicked the cigarette down and twisted his toe over the butt.

"I'm not yellow. What would Adrienne think of you playing around out here, putting your life at risk for a specter?" Wyatt thought about the thing and how it could be a wild animal.

Birdseed disregarded the sentiment. "She's tough."

Wyatt didn't want to argue about it. He also didn't want any rumors spreading about him being a coward. In a town where everyone knew everyone else's business, he'd rather not have something like that hanging over his head every time he wanted to buy a case of Stag at the local My-T-Mart. He clicked his flashlight on and pointed it at the ground.

The grass shifted under their feet, and to Wyatt's relief, Birdseed kept his mouth shut during the rest of the journey. Their twin spotlights wiggled over the terrain as they walked. The once-tiny glow in the distance grew and grew as they got closer to it. Birdseed approached the light, which sat encased in a small cage that was affixed to a pole stretching from a small, gated platform.

"Well, I'll be damned," Birdseed muttered, rubbing his chin. "It's an old elevator for a mine."

"I didn't know Royal Lake had a working mine." Wyatt shuffled toward the light for a closer view.

"Me neither. What do you suppose is feeding the energy to this light? I didn't think any power came out this far in the sticks."

"You're asking *me*? Who knows?" Wyatt shrugged.

Birdseed pulled out another cigarette from a front pocket. He tipped the box toward Wyatt with an inquisitive expression, but Wyatt scrunched his nose and pursed his lips, declining the offer.

"Your face looks like a butthole when you do that," Birdseed said.

"Whatever. What is that, number three since we've been out here?"

Birdseed ignored him. When he lit the end, the flicker of the orange light illuminated not only his face but also the immediate area. They stood on a thick metal plate with an engraving on the top.

"Oh, neat. Look at that," Birdseed said, blowing out smoke and scraping his toe across the old engraving.

"Whoa, this is old... I mean, really old...like centuries old," Wyatt said. He bent down and picked at part of the engraving. Hard mud had been packed into the finer details.

"No way, not centuries. Wouldn't we have known about this?"

Wyatt shrugged. "I have no idea, but I don't like this. It's giving me the creeps. Why would this light come on all of a sudden after all these years of this place being abandoned with no one in town knowing it's here? Where's the rest of the mine?"

"Well, I would guess we're standing on it. I bet this plate is actually the elevator floor. Man, how cool would it be to see what the mine looks like now... I wonder if that thing we saw went down here."

"I don't know, 'seed..." Wyatt bit his lip as he shifted his weight.

"Hmm, you look an awful shade of...yellow." Birdseed grinned.

"Shut up. I'm no coward." Sweat beaded up on Wyatt's brow. He knew his friend wouldn't tarnish his name, but he wasn't sure who could be listening to their conversation.

Chuckling, Birdseed flicked ash at the light. "Let's go then. It's Mulberry's problem."

As the men shuffled back toward the woods, restlessness stirred in Wyatt. All his life, he'd lived in Birdseed's skinny, smoky shadow. He wanted his friend to know that he wasn't a scared puddle of chunky mush, so he stopped in his tracks.

"No, man, we can mess with it tomorrow when it's daylight." Birdseed stopped and turned, sighing.

"I want to see it now. And…find out if that thing went down there," Wyatt said, voice trembling, "We ran all the way out here for a suspicious entity, and we found a clue."

Birdseed groaned and kicked the grass. "Fine," he muttered, clicking on his flashlight. He jittered the beam across the ground back toward the elevator. Wordlessly, the men crept back to the mine as the pit in Wyatt's stomach grew.

He wondered if he was making a mistake, but the risk of the unknown wasn't nearly as great as the risk of being the town shmuck. As they stood back on the ornate metal plating, Birdseed wrapped his hands around the pole of the light. Using his flashlight, he scanned over the pole to find the controls. There it was: a small caged button between the railing and light.

"Ah, here's a switch," he said. A surge in the electrical feed pulsed, causing the bulb to flicker. He looked at Wyatt. "Are you sure?"

Wyatt wasn't sure. "Just push it already," he said, wringing his hands as he rocked over the balls of his feet. The anticipation stung like rot in his belly as Birdseed jammed his thumb over the little red circle. A small click followed by a weak whir made the men perk up. "There's still power! Press it again," he said.

"I told you I think this thing is sealed up. It probably doesn't matter if this control works or not. If it's sealed, it's sealed."

Wyatt nudged him out of the way and examined the red knob. A quick press triggered the same click and whir. Wyatt pushed it over and over, bobbing his head with each press as if willing the motor to pry the platform from centuries of caked-in mud and rust.

"It's sealed, Wyatt..." Birdseed lit another cigarette and let it hang from his lip.

Wyatt shot him a defiant stare. "The fourth one now?" He squeezed the button over and over, locking eyes with him. The mechanism whirred on the sixteenth push, but this time, it was followed by a jarring *thunk*. As the platform shook, both men grabbed the support rail to keep from meeting the ground.

"Oh, damn," Birdseed said, gripping the rail with the cigarette bobbing from his mouth. He kicked some of the dust from the plate.

Wyatt used the full force of the pad of his thumb to punch the button and hold it down. The platform rocked back and forth with a jolt, and then the gears smoothed out, ferrying them into the depths of the earth.

"Ha! Sealed in my ass." Wyatt smiled and gave Birdseed the finger.

While they descended into the hole, they scanned the area, trying to make out their surroundings in pitch black.

"I still think we should have waited until morning. I'm starting to doubt the idea of wandering around in an old mine in the middle of the night," Birdseed said, ignoring Wyatt's crude gesture.

"You're just *now* starting to doubt? What was that? Oh, right... What could be down here to be afraid of? We have our weapons, right?" Wyatt mocked his friend, raising an eyebrow. "Or are you the one pissing your drawers now?"

Birdseed waved his hand in dismissal and crushed the cigarette under his boot.

"Good idea," Wyatt remarked. "We don't know what kinds of built-up gases might be down here."

"Only the ones coming from your mouth. And probably"—he craned his neck toward Wyatt's backside—"back there."

"Har-har."

The elevator continued its descent as the mine opened itself up to them. They surveyed the opening with their flashlights, sending white circles over craggy surfaces and rotted support beams. Tiny veils of dust sprinkled from various cracks in the ceiling.

"Wait, what's that?" Birdseed pointed his light in the distance in front of them. Their eyes adjusted to the blackness, and they were able to spot another dim light deeper in the cavern.

"No way someone's down here. No *way*!" Wyatt said. He was flicking his light around the perimeter of the cavern when the elevator lurched. They stumbled into the support rail, looking toward the ground. "Oh Lord..."

Wyatt shot a glance up and saw one of the cables spinning erratically, making *ping! ping! n*oises as it uncoiled down to its last rusted thread. He opened his mouth into a large *O* before the cable snapped, sending the men plummeting toward the ground.

"Oh, crap! Oh, god!" Birdseed jumped up and down, hoping to lessen the blow of the fall. Wyatt said nothing as he, too, jumped up and down.

As the platform slapped the ground, their knees crumpled, sending them into the dirt and rolling from the lift. Groaning, Wyatt moved to his side, thankful their sidearms didn't go off into their meaty cheeks. Or worse...their jewels.

Birdseed lifted his arm and studied his wrist. "Son of a—" His arm bent at a weird angle. He attempted to roll his wrist, but it couldn't be done.

"Oh, man. Oh, man, I'm so sorry, man! What can I do? What do you need?"

"Hell, I don't know... Got any aspirin?" Birdseed cupped his forehead and winced. He lifted himself from the ground, holding his wrist and peering up through the chute they'd careened down. He sucked air through his teeth as he unbuttoned his uniform shirt and attempted to sling his arm in it.

"Damn it, we aren't getting out of here, are we?" Wyatt ran his fingers through his hair, gripping chunks while gritting his teeth.

"Not now, we're not," Birdseed grunted painfully, "We'll have to wait until daylight. Then we can figure out our escape."

"Daylight? How would we even know if it's daylight down here?"

"Duh, Wyatt. We just made a big hole with the elevator."

"Did you bring your phone? Can you call Adrienne?"

Birdseed reached into his back pocket and pulled out a small, older flip phone. When he opened it, the hinge shattered, and the screen had cracked to oblivion. He tried to trigger the power, but nothing happened.

"Crap. What about yours?"

Wyatt held up a shattered Android.

Birdseed nodded and called into his radio. Static. Wyatt copied him and got the same static.

"There must be lead in the dirt," Birdseed said, half joking.

"This is *not* cool."

"Well, I'd say we're in quite the pickle." Birdseed scratched his chin while jutting out his jaw.

The darkness folded in on Wyatt, making him shiver. Goosebumps swelled on his arms, and he snapped in a panic. He jumped in front of Birdseed, nearly touching his nose with his own. "How are you staying so calm about all this? We're trapped in a dark mine that's God knows how old, with whoever the hell is down here breathing in all the dust and old gas in the place!"

"Whoa. Say it, don't spray it."

"I should have swallowed my pride and walked away from this death trap!" He paced around, his feet splayed outward, making him look like a frantic duck.

Birdseed huffed. "There's no sense in flipping out, man. We're already in a jam—we don't need to add more stress to the situation." He tried to raise his injured arm but failed. "Besides, *I'm* the one with the broken arm. If there's some predator down here, they're going to have a nice meal of Birdseed."

Wyatt leered at his friend. "But..." He lowered his voice, "I'm meatier." He took a deep breath and rubbed the extra flesh pooling around his waistband.

Against his better judgment, he knew nothing could be done standing around, so he whispered, "Do you want to see what that room is all about?"

Birdseed nodded. "Yep. We've got nothing else to do. Maybe the cave dweller will have a splint for my busted arm."

They clicked on their flashlights and scanned the ground. As their steps echoed in the cavern, occasionally, Birdseed pointed his light toward the ceiling to check for rogue bats. He shuddered every time as if anticipating a dive bomb. Wyatt remembered when they were kids, exploring old Silver Lake like they had millions of times before; a bat had flown down into Birdseed's mess of puffy hair. It was tangled pretty good in his auburn curls, flapping and screeching and pooping on his head. Wyatt had to use his pocketknife to cut it free, nicking Birdseed's head in the process. When he thought more about it, he wondered if that's when everyone started calling him Birdseed. Shouldn't it have been bird *nest*? Or bat nest? Wyatt shrugged.

The lit room became more vibrant as they approached, and the faint sound of a banjo over soft static flowed into the space.

"Is that a *radio* in there? I..." Wyatt gulped hard. "I have so many questions."

"Sounds like it. Although I have no idea how they get a signal down here."

Wyatt shrugged again and became more intentional with his steps the closer they got. Once they reached the source of the light, they realized a small cave had been carved into the side of the shaft, with a single bulb stolen from another area and strung up in the middle of a makeshift bedroom. He peered inside the musty cave to see a single mattress covered in dark stains and a table along the wall. The table contained the radio and a single open notebook with a pen lying across the pages.

"What the hell?" Birdseed whispered, sliding his pistol from the holster. "Someone lives down here."

Little bumps prickled on Wyatt's skin, and he was ready to crawl up the side of the mine shaft, elevator be damned. "We need to leave. *Now.*"

"How exactly are we going to do that?" Birdseed didn't look at Wyatt, keeping his barrel trained around the perimeter of the room. "Right now, the only thing that can fly out of here is a bird or a bug or a—"

"Bat..." The voice came from behind Wyatt, and he jumped, pinching off the tiny dribble of pee that had squirted out. He grabbed Birdseed's arm, forgetting it was broken.

Birdseed hissed in pain, swinging his pistol around to point it at the figure in the doorway.

"Who are you?" the sheriff demanded.

The figure stood stupidly in front of them. "Who'm I? Who're *you?*" the man responded and pointed a slender finger down to the first knuckle in the barrel of Birdseed's gun. He popped it back out, and it made a funny noise.

Wyatt's heart skipped a beat, and he swallowed, looking back to his friend for direction. Birdseed eyed the man, then decided to put his gun away. That didn't sit well with Wyatt, even if the gun didn't faze the man.

The stranger's brown eyes drifted outward as if trying to get a good look at his temples. He wore only a dirty gray cloth that hung on him like a potato sack torn to ribbons at the edges. He stood with his arms at his sides like an ape, his knobby knees pointing toward each other. As he stuck out his lower jaw, the soft sounds of Conway Twitty echoed from the radio in the bedroom behind them.

"I...I'm, uh..." The eyes drifted farther outward and bugged out a little. "I...I'm Birdseed, and this is my buddy, Wyatt."

"*Birdseed*," he snorted. "What th' hell kinda name is that?"

He shrugged, "That's what they call me. And you are...?"

"Names, names... There ain't no names here. But yeh can call me *Big Greasy* if yeh wan'." As he said the name, he smeared something from his other hand over the potato sack shirt, leaving a dark, smudgy trail. Wyatt scrunched his nose.

"Big...Greasy? Ah, okay, that's a little weird, but I'll go with it."

"Um, M-mister...uh...Greasy," Wyatt stuttered while stepping forward and hovering his hand over his taser. "Do you ever get out of this mine?"

"Hah! *Mis*-ter Greasy! You make me soun' like one eh them fancy folk from way back when." He glared at Wyatt, lowering his voice to growl. "I ain't one eh them fancy folk." He shoved past the pair into the room and moved toward the desk with the notebook. He then sat down and began to write, ignoring them.

Birdseed and Wyatt exchanged glances. "Uh, Big Greasy," Birdseed said. "You mind if I just call you Greasy? You didn't answer the question... Do you ever get out of here?"

The odd man rose up like a squirrel, then slapped his pen down on the journal. "Th' thing is, I jus' ate, and I don't *need* ya! Lemme write this down. Then I'll pay attention to yeh whiny pricks."

Wyatt's jaw dropped as he expressed shock at his friend. He raised his hands and mouthed, "O-kay."

They stepped out of the makeshift room to study the cavern for a way out. Wyatt leaned in to whisper, "This guy is not right. I doubt he can help us out of this mine... He was probably born down here for all we kn—"

"A'right, yeh sad sacks." Big Greasy sauntered out of his room. "Follow me." He waved a bony arm as he moved through the cavern, passing the broken elevator.

With a shrug, Birdseed followed with Wyatt firmly at his heels. He didn't like this. He lit the walls with his flashlight beam while trying to come up with a plan in case things went sour. Big Greasy hunched as he walked, swaying his arms like a skinny monkey. His bare feet slapped against the uneven stone ground.

Wyatt found it odd that the man was neither bothered by their presence in his mine shaft nor excited for company. There was no doubt Big Greasy hadn't seen the light of day in decades, let alone another human. Life in solitude could do that to a man. Maybe he had become so accustomed to his own company that being introduced to a new person was less inviting and more of a nuisance. At least, that was what Wyatt wanted to tell himself.

The soft banjo music faded as they continued deeper into the cavern. Wyatt's skin chilled the darker their surroundings became. The darker the surroundings, the more erratic his flashlight beam. He had warmed up to the music in the room, and it became a slice of comfort while they stood in the awkward and uneasy presence of Big Greasy. And now it was fading away, just like any semblance of peace he could have had. Birdseed continued to scan the walls with his light, holding his arm against his chest in an effort to immobilize it.

"Well, here it is." Big Greasy came to a halt, his flipper feet slapping down on the rocks.

Birdseed almost crashed into the back of him. "Here *what* is?" he asked, squeezing his arm even closer to his body.

"Yer exit, dummy. This's where I come n' go." Big Greasy pointed a long finger up toward an opening in the ceiling. A peek of moonlight glimmered over and through the hole, illuminating the man's almost transparent flesh.

Wyatt noticed a change in Big Greasy revealed only by the moonlight. How did he miss the trace of dark veins under the skin, spreading like spiderwebs up his arm and through the flesh of his face? A feral glow lit the back of his eyes, making eerie traces over Birdseed without his notice. Those damn goosebumps again. Was this the creature they'd seen in the woods?

"Well?" Big Greasy shrugged and gestured at the hole.

"What, are you going to hoist us up there and hope we can fly the rest of the way? How do you get up there?" Birdseed paid no attention to Big Greasy as he scanned the environment and focused on his broken arm and the peephole in the ceiling.

A grin crept across the man's pallid, vein-flecked face. Wyatt's heart thumped in his chest. He took a step back while the sound of his blood squeezing in and out of his arteries filled his ears with a high-pitched liquid squeal. He didn't hear Birdseed; he shook and wanted to run.

A tiny sliver of clarity opened up his hearing, and it was Big Greasy. "Here, lemme help yeh!" The man leapt like a spider before landing on Birdseed's shoulders. He bent down and clamped hard on his neck, spraying Wyatt's uniform with a webbing of dark maroon. His big blue eyes glistened with shock, and fear stole all the moisture from his mouth. He nearly lost his bladder as his tongue raked dry against his soft palate. He watched his friend spinning in circles, trying to buck off the backcountry underground mine dweller.

Wyatt bounced, whimpering like a child— a scared, childish coward, as he raced away from his only friend. Once the blood had run from his head to fuel his legs, he heard Birdseed thump to the ground in the distance. His friend's voice echoed off the walls. "Ow! Damn it!"

He didn't want to stick around to check whether he was dead—he ran. Wyatt puffed and puffed as he jogged around the mine, not knowing where his feet would fall or whether an ankle-twisting trap waited for him somewhere along the path. His flashlight jerked frantic circles over the cave walls.

"Hee-hee heeeeee! Here, piggy, piggy!" Big Greasy giggled maniacally. Wyatt felt the breeze of the man's breath on his neck.

"I'm not that fat!" Wyatt wheezed through his sprinting, peering over his shoulder and seeing no one. Confused, he slowed to a jog, then stopped to bend over and catch his breath.

A childish giggle echoed through the cavern. Wyatt grappled for his pistol, yanking it from the holster. "Don't come any closer!" His voice trembled, giving away his fear. He expected to see Big Greasy crawling over the walls like some hillbilly spider.

Wyatt stood still, knees locked and knocking. While scanning the walls and hearing distant laughter, he suddenly felt sad. The thought of his old grade school friend being murdered by that lanky mess of limbs and dirt made his stomach hurt. Birdseed's real name was James, but no one had called him that in years. He was probably the last person to know that, except Adrienne.

"Damn redneck," he whispered to no one, lowering his gun.

"I ain't no redneck." As the voice hit Wyatt's left ear, his bladder loosened. He spun around, face-to-face, with lazy eyes and a slack jaw.

"Boo!"

Wyatt screamed and turned to run, but the creature from the woods perched upon his shoulders, weighing him down. He felt a prick on his neck when he fell to the ground.

2

STRANDED

"DANG IT, JACE! WHY do you *insist* on not taking care of your car?" Kennedy Jones burst from the passenger seat and slapped the smoking hood of the cream-colored sedan. Her boyfriend, Jace, triggered the latch and slid from the driver's side to join her. He stood tall and lanky next to her petite frame.

"I guess I should have gotten that oil change six months ago," he said, scratching his head. Thick blond waves wiggled under his fingers as he frowned.

"Six *months* ago? I swear, you can be so helpless sometimes." Blue plumes of smoke belched from the engine as she propped up the hood and peered inside.

She groaned, dispersing the smoke with a flailing hand. They were stranded in the middle of a two-way country highway with only the distant smoky hills and rows of sunflowers and alfalfa to call to for help. The sun blazed overhead. Kennedy pulled out her phone and saw she had no signal. She knew it had to be the curtain of trees packed on either side of the road that was eating the signal.

"Are you getting a signal at all?" she asked, holding her phone high, hoping to catch a low-hanging wave.

Jace also pulled out his phone. He swung it around, poked it in the air, then drew it close to his nose. "No, nothing."

"Damn it, I knew we shouldn't have taken this shortcut. Now, we'll never get to see Tool live! We've wasted two hundred bucks and however much more now that the car's busted." She slammed the hood down, pounding a fist over the thin metal. Putting her hands on her hips, she turned to Jace, who shrugged.

"I'm sorry. I forget about stuff like that sometimes." He strolled behind her and wrapped his arms around her waist. "How about I make it up to you later?" He nuzzled his face into her still-cool neck.

Kennedy grunted. "I don't know how, but I'll come up with something you won't forget." She smiled and leaned into him. Turning her head, she pecked him on the lips. "For now, we need to figure out how to get to a town to fix your stupid car."

She pulled his arms from around her waist and pointed down the road. "Let's walk a little way and see if either of us can get a signal."

After hoisting their bags across their backs, they locked up the smoking sedan and wandered north. Kennedy had many thoughts about her feelings toward Jace's lackadaisical approach to life. He always overlooked something as simple as basic vehicle maintenance unless she reminded him. She glanced at him as they walked, his hand planked against his brow and looking forward with a squint. He paid no attention to her walking beside him. As in life, he had blinders on, only seeing what was directly in front of him. His sense of humor kept her around. It also didn't hurt his case that his fuse was so long that she wasn't sure if it even had an end, which helped temper her own anger at times.

The sun beat down on the pair, creating dark, wet circles on their shirts. Time mercilessly crawled as each footfall felt like an eternity.

"Does no one ever come down this road?" Kennedy complained, wiping a slick of sweat from her brow.

Jace opened his mouth to speak when the deep rumbling of a truck growled from behind. "Speak of the Devil," he said, nudging Kennedy.

He turned and waved his arms at the red beater bouncing over the ripples in the pavement. It slowed down next to them.

On the edge of the window rested a thick, tanned arm attached to a portly middle-aged man. He grinned at the pair with yellowed, crooked teeth and a toothpick hanging from his lip. The brim of a red ball cap shaded his eyes. The driver had the same general appearance but skinnier. The truck backfired, and Kennedy jumped, grabbing Jace.

"Well, what're y'all doin' out here in the middle a'nowhere?" the larger man emphasized the "wh"s of his words, sending whooshing beats from inwardly sunken lips. Jace stood in front of Kennedy, but she rocked back and forth on her toes to peek over his shoulders.

"Why are they talking like that?" she whispered in his ear.

Jace waved her away. "Car trouble. Is there a town nearby with a shop?" he asked.

Not giving the pair an answer right away, the man eyeballed them up and down. An uncomfortable silence brewed in Kennedy's gut, causing her to wring her hands. A strong aroma of warm, salty sunscreen wafted into her nostrils.

"Sure do," he said, licking his lips. "It's just a few miles up ahead. We can take you'ns that way if ya like."

Jace peered at Kennedy, who was rubbing her sweat-salted face into her shirt. She nodded while continuing to dig at the water pooled in the corner of her eye.

"Ain't no room in the cab— mind ridin' in the back?" The man jabbed his thumb toward the bed of the truck.

Jace tilted his head toward the bed of the truck. Kennedy walked to the back and peered inside. Tufts of fur and traces of gore had settled in the grooves of the bed liner. The hair prickled on her neck, and she turned to Jace with a grimace. He noticed as well, mirroring her expression.

"I don't want you to walk for miles in this heat, Kay," he whispered to her. Without her approval, he shouted to the men in the cabin. "No problem. Thanks for your help!"

Jace lifted Kennedy inside, then gave her a pinch on the rear before climbing in after her. She swatted his shoulder and giggled. Her laughter was cut short when she surveyed the truck bed to find a place to sit that was free of hair clods and meat. Her smile curved down, and she sighed.

The truck backfired, making her yelp, and she forced a laugh as she plopped down on the bump of the wheel. They didn't talk too much after that, with the wailing breeze over their ears and the rumbling engine drowning out all other sounds. Fat tires crunched over the freshly oiled pavement, kicking up the pungent aroma of black grease. Jace sat closer to the door flap, one knee up with an elbow crossed over, hand dangling. His other hand rested on his face, one thumb under his chin and forefinger rubbing his lip. Kennedy called this his "thinker pose." When not in conversation, Jace drifted away in thought to places he would never share, which Kennedy found a touch annoying. She never pressed him about it, though.

After what seemed like forever sitting in the filthy truck and enduring a never-ending sinus punch of oil and dirt, the pair sighed as the truck ground to a halt in the dusty lot of a hybrid auto shop and gas station with a convenience store.

"Douglas Auto and My-T-Mart," Kennedy read the signs aloud. Plumes of dust rose on either side of the truck.

Jace stood up and stuck out a hand for her. She rose with him and stretched her arms up in the air. Jace took another glance at the truck bed, toeing at a hair clod. It turned over, revealing jellied clotting and bits of flesh. His skin rippled, and he shuddered, goose flesh tingling the surface.

The tanned, portly fellow from the passenger side unhooked the hatch without a word. He chewed on his toothpick and winked at Kennedy, who stopped stretching and slowly wrapped her arms around her chest.

"That there is yer auto shop." The man pointed to Douglas Auto. "And that there is yer convenience shop."

"Thanks, man." Jace stuck out a hand, and the man stared down at it, hand firmly stuck in his pocket. He gave a short grin and tipped his ball cap. "Yeah, yeah. Now go on and git. I gotta get down to my waterin' hole."

He didn't have to ask Kennedy twice. She flew from the truck bed and scurried toward Douglas Auto.

The man in the red hat turned on his heel and slid back into the truck. It backfired again, but rather than jump, Jace stared at the truck as it disappeared in a cloud of yellow dust.

***

An old brass bell fixed with fraying twine rolled around on the doorframe as Kennedy slid through the crack in the opening she made to Douglas Auto. A man in overalls lay slumped over the counter; ball cap tipped halfway over his balding head and unaware of her presence. No one else was in the small auto repair shop. The place held a strong aroma of Coppertone and cigarette smoke, making her wriggle her nose. A radio crackled on the counter, playing the same Earl Scruggs tune she remembered hearing through the back window of the truck that had brought them here.

I hate country music. Kennedy clamped her teeth and surveyed the room.

The waiting room consisted of two plastic folding chairs around an old fruit crate posing as a side table. She eyed the man again, hoping he was asleep and not actually dead. She didn't want to try rousing him without Jace with her, so she wandered toward a chair and stopped short of its splattered brown surface. She took in a sharp breath and folded her arms. A tube TV hummed in the corner with the local news running.

"The annual county fair has been set up, and our guests from the hill are gearing up for the demo derby tonight! All the townies have already begun to crowd the field…" The newscaster had a more professional twang and wore a button-up collared light-blue flannel shirt. He continued to buzz in the background.

Jace popped open the door, clanging the brass bell, and the man behind the counter snorted, rising and blinking slowly. Kennedy swung her head toward the entrance and breathed a sigh of relief when she realized the man was alive.

"Oh, pardon me, sir…missus." The man smacked his lips and rubbed his eyes. "S'been a long week. How can I help yeh?"

Jace strolled toward the counter with Kennedy at his heels. "Yeah, we had a little trouble down the road that way," he said, stabbing his thumb behind his shoulder. "Our car broke down in the middle of the road."

"Is that right?" the man peered at the couple. He sighed and brushed his oily, calloused hands over his overalls. "I ken probably help yeh, but seein' as it's the county fair goin' on, it might be a few days before I ken get any parts. I'll send my guy to give her a tow. I'll know more when he gets back."

Kennedy groaned. "A few *days*?"

Jace placed an arm around the small of her back and drew her closer to him. He did this often to staunch her temper.

"Yeh. I mean, if it needs parts I don't got anyway. If it don't need 'em, or I got 'em already, I ken get 'er done by tomorrow."

Jace turned to Kennedy. "We don't have much choice. I mean, having us back on the road tomorrow isn't that bad."

"Well, tha's if I don' need to order nothin'," the mechanic interrupted. "By the way, name's Otis. People 'round here call me Gearhead."

Gearhead seemed like a likable guy. "Okay, well, how soon can your man tow my car to the shop?" asked Jace.

"Eh, he ken do it now. Won't take long. Why don' you take it easy over at the café 'cross the road? I'll call yeh when I figure out wha's wrong. Need yer keys, though." Gearhead held out his thick palm.

Jace fumbled in his pocket, pulled out the fob, and plunked it into Gearhead's outstretched hand. The old man examined the fob and rocked the keychain in his hand, jangling it about. "Yeh, say i's jus' down the road?" Gearhead pointed a thick finger in the direction of where they'd come from.

"Yes, that's right. I don't know the name of the road, but I remember sunflowers and alfalfa."

"Right. Leave yer number and I'll call when I figure out wha's wrong." He tapped on a little pad of Post-its and motioned to the cup of pens nearby. Leaving the pair, he turned his back and wandered through the door behind the counter.

Jace turned to Kennedy, who had her arms crossed and wore a deep frown. He shrugged. "We don't have a choice, babe. Maybe this is a sign we didn't belong at the concert..."

"Was it a sign that we would be out this much money? That seems unfair."

"Ah, don't worry about it." He moved his arm from Kennedy's back to her shoulders, pulling her closer to kiss the top of her head. "I'll work overtime for some extra money. I'm sure Don will let me. He's always asking for volunteers."

"If you say so," she huffed, her voice muffled in Jace's armpit.

"Let's head over to that café." He grabbed her by the hand and tugged her outside the auto shop, and they were once again in the dusty parking lot. Sure enough, a small café sat right across the narrow road.

3

These Little Feet

Birdseed scratched his shoulder and shuddered. A thin veil of dust shimmied from the ceiling, and particles floated through the air across yellow incandescence. The radio crackled and hummed with a fine riff of banjo licks.

"Yo, we 'bout ready fer later?" Wyatt scratched his ass, then rubbed his face.

Birdseed grimaced. "Gross." He replied, staring at his friend.

"Wut?"

"Ner'mind. Yeah, I got 'er planned. Should be lot'er folks tonight. Got some jars fer leftovers. Adrienne's got a freezer." Birdseed rapped a finger against a box of clean Mason jars on the table before he stood up and stretched. His thin white tee was speckled with gray, brown, and splatters of maroon he'd tried to scrub out. As he stretched, the outline of his rib cage rippled beneath the fabric, and he nearly lost his pants. "Whoops!" he said, clawing at the hem and pulling it back over his hips.

"I'm so hungry..." Wyatt groaned, rubbing the spot where he once had a nice, round tummy. It was gone now-- replaced by a gaunt grayness and constant rumble of starvation.

"Me too. Ain't nothin' we can do till later, so be patient. You got yer cream?"

Wyatt stared off into the corner. A pile of blanched bones lay crumpled in a heap there, draped over by an old gray potato-sack-like covering that was shredded near the bottom.

"How many times yeh gonna stare at 'em?" Birdseed raked his tongue across a freshly drawn cigarette before sticking it between his lips.

"How many times yeh gonna keep smokin' them damn things?"

Birdseed shrugged.

Wyatt sighed. "Sorry. I just... I'm jus' still tryin' ta figure out why it din't work right."

"Wut? Killin' 'im?"

"Yeh. I mean, don' all vamps go back ta normal once their...ye know...maker dies?"

"It ain't the movies, dumbass." Birdseed lit the end of the cigarette before taking a long drag and studying his friend.

"Hey, you thought it too."

"I was a dumbass too. B'sides, you read the journal. I don' know if we really is vamps."

Wyatt stared at the frayed edges of the old journal. The paper inside was brittle and smelled weird. The beginning of the journal was written in such fine script that he could barely read it. Something about a busted wagon wheel and a trap. He never would have guessed Big Greasy was a pioneer.

Nehemiah was his name. He had a family and a dream of starting a ranch out west, but he never made it past Royal Lake, Alabama.

"Yeh din't answer me. Yeh got yer cream?"

Wyatt snapped out of his daydream. "Yeah, yeah, I got it."

Birdseed sighed. "C'mon, man. Stop thinkin' 'bout 'im."

Wyatt ignored him and went back to the journal. He flipped through the pages, watching the fine penmanship of ages ago morph into the crazed scrawlings of a madman.

After a gang of roving bandits attacked Nehemiah's caravan, they killed his wife and two daughters, taking all they had. The bandits spared him, leaving him to shoulder the grief alone in the dirt, still on his knees, begging for their lives. Wyatt read the words again.

> *Doth the Lord despise His servant? Am I not worthy of Thy blessings? Oh, Hannah. Oh, Dora. Oh, Claudine! If I am not worthy in Thy presence, and I am damned either way, then it is the Devil I now seek!*

Wyatt felt bad for him. Didn't he know the story of Job? He could only guess that Big Greasy had made a bargain with Lucifer himself to become whatever that was. He glanced at the pile of bones again. Whatever "that" was had turned him and his buddy into whatever they now were.

After his pact, Nehemiah had fed on squirrels and raccoons, hiding in dark spaces under cover of night in shame, until the mining company that owned this place eventually abandoned it. It was then he took up residence here, leaving the company of men behind and slowly turning into a starving, infectious creature who loved Conway Twitty. Wyatt raised an eyebrow; he kinda liked Conway too. He turned the page over to Big Greasy's final entry.

> *Hee-hee! Oh, me! Oh, my! I caught me some real'uns tonight! I ken smell 'em and I ken taste 'em now. I'ma turn 'em an' make em ma frens! Skibbidy beep beep bop!*

Wyatt rolled his eyes. If he knew what he was writing the day they'd met, he would have plugged him then and there. Now, all he could do was thank the pile of bones for his new "accent," among other things.

He knew he was sensitive to light. Of course he would be. Any pact with the Devil would be a descent into darkness. Big Greasy was very old, and Wyatt was afraid of immortality. His body had become nothing but bones, with a hunger that could never be slaked. He tried to hang himself behind Birdseed's back, but it didn't work. He tried to shoot himself in the temple, and that didn't work either. Birdseed found out about that one and was pretty pissed at him for a while, so he didn't try again.

As far as he knew, Big Greasy was a few hundred years old. Whatever magic had kept him alive had been snuffed out when he and Birdseed had lopped off his head. If Wyatt could only get someone to chop off his head, he could be free... Unless there was another way.

Birdseed blew out a long stream of air, almost like a whistle, and shook his head. "We gotta do better this time."

"What do yeh mean?" Wyatt came out of his daydream, barely hearing the question.

"Gotta finish 'em off. Ain't leavin' none alive like las' year. Whole town's gone hungry now. I hate meself fer turnin' Adrienne."

Hungry. There was a time not long ago, but ages ago, when Wyatt could eat whatever he wanted. And that meant food...*real* food. In his other life, people had made fun of his gut, and he'd always try to counter his food addiction by running, lifting weights, doing the ThighMaster...but none of them had made him skinny like Big Greasy's kiss. Now, he'd die to get his pudge back.

"Preserves is good, though."

"It's not the same. 'Member, don't be shootin' 'em like yeh did las' year. We need ta' collect as much as we ken carry an' shootin's wasteful."

Wyatt sighed. "Wish we'd nev'r come down tha' elevator."

"True. True. 'Cuz then we coulda still been livin' up top." Birdseed nodded. "Where Adrienne is."

"Well, she's stuck in that ol' diner now."

"Better than here."

"I's safer down here. No light...is nice an cold..." Wyatt stuck his arms out.

Birdseed huffed and gave him a real bird.

"Hey, now, yeh still get ta see her! She loves yeh and always waits for yeh. I don' got no one but you."

Birdseed cracked a small smile and draped an arm around Wyatt's shoulder. "An' I'm just tha *best!*" His auburn curls bobbed around as the smoke trail crept up over his face. Wyatt waved his hand and pursed his lips, making a show of holding his breath.

"Ain't gonna kill me now, is it?" Birdseed clicked his tongue and winked, letting go of Wyatt.

He wasn't wrong. The hunger drove Wyatt mad, but his conscience drove him madder. He hated killing people, but he had to. Birdseed didn't mind as much, saying it was a necessary evil. He didn't like the horrifying noises folks made when they died, though. Still, he muscled through it every time, reasoning that turning half the town into rabid hillbillies was a fate worse than death.

"You 'bout ready?" Birdseed licked a finger and wiped it on his shirt. He'd changed into his "clean" outfit for the show.

"Yeah, I'm ready."

The pair strolled out of the room with the box of Mason jars and other supplies in a sling bag. Once they saw the light's soft haze glinting off the cavern wall, Birdseed set the sack down. He glanced up at the ceiling and saw all the brown wriggling teardrops hanging there.

"Of all things ta turn into, it's gotta be a damn bat," he scoffed.

Without another word, they shrank into their travel forms. With both sets of tiny feet, they grabbed the sling bag and rose through the hole.

4

PIES, MADE IN-HOUSE

KENNEDY SHUFFLED ALONGSIDE JACE toward the little restaurant across from Douglas Auto. A crudely cobbled wooden sign dangled from the window with bold red paint: Ho Made Pies. The corner of the sign thunked against the window in the light breeze.

"Mmmm, just how I like my pies... 'ho' made," Kennedy said, sniggering.

Jace snorted. "Think they make them with that special slut crust?"

When they opened the door, the creak it made could have woken the dead. The few patrons inside turned to look at them, and the room went silent. Pink rose in Kennedy's cheeks as Jace, ever the calm one, led her toward a two-seater next to a couple of men leaning back in their chairs. One man's chair looked about to give out underneath him, while the other man's slender frame was swallowed by his own chair.

Every noise Jace and Kennedy made in the establishment ricocheted off the walls and drew attention to them. From the act of pulling out the chairs with their prolonged skidding across the floor to settling into the squeaking wooden seats, they triggered many glances to their spot. The two men next to them didn't mind them and continued their conversation.

"Welcome to Pappy's. I'm Adrienne. What'll it be, hon?" The waitress, no older than nineteen, approached their table. She didn't look like she belonged in this town. Her dark hair was tied up in a low bun, and she had an athletic build. She peered at them with striking hazel eyes and not a blemish on her porcelain skin. An old-school pad of paper rested in her hand, with a pencil tip poised on the surface, waiting for their orders. The overturned piece of paper over her fingers flapped from the fan blowing in the upper corner of the ceiling.

"Oh! I uh-uh...do you serve coffee here?" Jace asked.

"Sure do. Cream and sugar?"

"No, just black, please. Oh, and what is your '*ho*' made pie of the day?" His lip quivered, and Kennedy put her face in her hands.

"Today's a foot-high lemon meringue. You want some?"

"Yes, please." His voice trembled while holding back the sniggering. He smiled at the waitress, pulling his lips together and blowing small raspberries as the laughter leaked from his mouth.

The waitress didn't seem to notice his jape and turned to Kennedy. "How 'bout you, hon?"

"Um, I'll have the same, please."

"Black coffee and pie then. All right, be right back."

Kennedy watched her go. The restaurant was heavy with the aroma of fried meats and sunscreen. "Why does this whole damn town smell like SPF fifty?" she whispered.

"Hm, I haven't really noticed," Jace responded, taking whiffs of the air. "Yeah, I guess it does smell like sunscreen."

She surveyed the dining room. No one was staring at them anymore, and the inside became a cacophony of twangy chatter. Kennedy caught snippets of conversation from the next table over.

"You ain't never been to no demo derby?" The large pink man with the weak chair next to them wore a stained, undersized white T-shirt. He scratched his belly.

"I told yeh I ain't nevah! But I wanna..." The rack of bones sharing his table rubbed a slim hand over the scruff of his chin.

The pink man was pink from a mixture of what looked to Kennedy like sunburn and gin blossoms. She wondered if he drank gin or just an overabundance of beer. He noticed her watching him. "How 'bout you, ma'am? You been t'a demo derby?"

Kennedy's hair prickled on her neck, and she realized she'd been staring at them. "I...I'm sorry, I wasn't trying to listen to your conversation." She kicked Jace under the table. He glared up at her and frowned.

"Aw, s'no worries. I was just tellin' my pal here how much fun they is."

She didn't know what to say. She didn't think they would invite her into their discussion. "Um, no...I haven't." She wanted them to forget she was there. Folding her arms, she narrowed her eyes at Jace, who glowered back at her while rubbing his shin.

"Oh, they's a good time. You should go! Good fortune you came across Royal Lake 'cuz the county fair is goin' on *right now*."

Jace continued to rub his shin. "Sounds like fun, but it depends on how long it takes your mechanic, Gearhead, to fix our car. I'm not sure we'll be able to stay up too late tonight in case he gets it done in the morning.."

"Ol' Gearhead? He's good people. Well, you should go to tha' fair at least. An' the derb is happenin' around two, so not too late. The fair's a good time," the skinny man said.

"Yeh, it's a *real* good time." The fatter man continued to rub his gut, stopping a moment to poke a finger into his belly button. "The fair's jus' down tha' road a bit. Here I ken draw yeh a map."

He pulled the napkin from under his glass and clicked a pen. The ink spread like tiny spider legs over the wet ring. He tossed the crudely drawn map onto their table, and the thin, waterlogged paper made a wet slap on the surface in front of Kennedy. Jace stared at the drawing. Adrienne came back and plopped the plate of pie over the map.

"Foot high indeed!" Kennedy said, poking the plate. The white meringue jiggled.

The fat man slapped his belly and sighed. "Welp, you'ns should go to the fair...and don't ferget yer *sunscreen*."

The odd way he said "sunscreen" unnerved Kennedy. *They must really be devoted to skin care in this town*, she thought. The sun was high, and the air was hot, so she understood to a point. The fact was, the smell was starting to niggle at her sinuses.

The men left, and the strange stink went with them. While Kennedy and Jace watched them leave, another couple slid inside the restaurant. The girl had long blond hair, perfectly straightened and shiny; it bounced as she moved. The man was tall and bald, with striking blue eyes. They looked like outsiders, just like her and Jace. The blonde caught Kennedy's eye and smiled. She tugged the bald man and walked toward their table.

"Hey, you guys aren't from around here, are you?" the woman asked, standing over their table. Kennedy slithered a hand over her pie as the stranger's wild, sparkling strands wiggled over their table, threatening to lose a thread and coil up onto her perfect meringue.

"Ah, no, we're not," Jace said, standing up to greet the new couple. He stuck out a hand, which the bald guy took. "I'm Jace, and this is my girlfriend, Kennedy. We're from Springfield."

The bald man nodded at the blonde. "This is my wife, Brooke, and I'm Kevin. Nice to meet you. We're also from Springfield."

"What a small world!" Kennedy chimed in. She pointed to the table the odd couple abandoned. "This table is free. I'd be careful, though. There was a rather large man in that chair—that one there—and it looks weak."

Brooke chuckled. "I'll sit in that one then. Kev, you sit there."

The couple took their seats.

"Ew, it's still warm," Brooke said. She flicked her hair behind her shoulder. It shimmered in the light filtering through the grimy front window. Kennedy was hypnotized by it and even a little jealous. Her plain brown hair sagged over her shoulders. She always had a halo of kinky frizz around her crown that she never knew how to manage.

Adrienne stopped by and attempted to hand them inkjet-printed menus on greasy copy paper.

"I'm actually in the mood for a big burger," Brooke said. "Just give me the biggest one you have."

Kevin smiled and shook his head. "I'll have the chicken fingers and fries."

Adrienne folded the menus and left with a strange, emotionless expression.

"Ooh, those look pretty good!" Brooke pointed at the slices of pie. "How are they?"

"We're about to find out," Kennedy said, poking her fork into the tip. The piece was too tall for the fork to capture the entire bite from top to bottom.

The metallic buzz of the fork hit her taste buds like a freight train, and her teeth chattered as her cheeks sucked inward. She let out a small grunt.

"I have a very strong sense of taste and smell," she told the couple. "It's got potential, but it's very tart."

"Maybe I'll pass," Brooke said, laughing. "I'll get something at the county fair."

"Oh, you're going to that?"

"Sure! That's why we're here."

The girl was very slender and petite. Kennedy wouldn't call her muscular or athletic, just slim. She wondered how a woman of her size would be able to stuff away a giant plate of a burger with fries while also tackling fair food. Despite being relatively small herself, she couldn't imagine eating that much in one sitting and then go to the fair and down loads of fried food.

The couple's orders' arrived shortly after that. "This looks *amazing*." Brooke clasped her hands and admired the burger for a moment before picking it up and practically unhinging her jaw to take the first bite. "It's been a long morning. I'm sooo hungry." She looked at Kennedy, her words muffled by a mix of bread, beef, and tomato. A speck of mustard clung to the corner of her mouth, which she daintily dabbed away.

In contrast, Kevin dipped his chicken fingers into the sauce so gingerly that Kennedy wondered if he got any sauce at all. She thought this was a couple she could get along with, and perhaps they could meet up sometime when they returned to Springfield."

"So why did you drive all the way out here for the county fair? Surely there are other entertaining things in Springfield," Kennedy said.

"Well, over the past couple of years, we've always heard, 'Go to the county fair at Royal Lake. It's so fun!' So Kev and I had some vacation time and thought we'd see what all the fuss was about. I don't have high expectations, though."

Kevin shrugged, still barely chewing his one bite of food. "What brings *you* here?"

"Well..." Jace dragged out the word, peering at Kennedy from the corner of his eye.

"Jace's car broke down on our way to the Tool concert," Kennedy interrupted. She nudged her foot against Jace's, this time more gently.

"Oh, bummer!" Brooke said. "I love Tool!"

Kennedy noticed her burger was already mostly gone. "Wow," she said. "Did you just suck that burger off the plate?"

"That's my little trash compactor," Kevin said, smiling.

"What?" Brooke shrugged with bread between her teeth.

"So, are you staying for the whole fair?" Jace asked.

Kevin nodded. "Yeah, we found a little KOA nearby, and we're going to camp out later after the demo derby."

"Ah, yes, the demo derby. We couldn't hear enough about *that*, could we?" Kennedy rolled her eyes toward Jace.

"Yeah, we hear it's a *real* good time." Jace narrowed his eyes, rubbed his stomach, and stuck a finger in his belly button.

Kennedy let out a loud guffaw. She clapped her hands over her mouth and continued to shake while laughing. Kevin and Brooke raised their eyebrows and looked back and forth at each other, then Jace.

Kennedy waved off her laughter. "Just something that happened earlier."

They sat with the couple for a while. Eventually, Kennedy learned that Brooke was a fermentation operator. She couldn't picture her tiny body moving around giant, three-thousand-liter industrial fermentation tanks with her long blond hair tucked into a regular-size hairnet. Brooke confirmed she wore three hairnets to contain her tresses. Now it made sense why she was able to eat so much, with all the sweating and climbing she did all day.

Kevin was a design engineer, spending most of his time sitting at a desk, creating models of medical devices. They had no kids yet but had only been married for a little less than a year.

"No kids yet, but any dogs or cats?" Kennedy asked.

"No...no pets either. We still live in a small apartment, saving up for our first down payment on a house. Real estate is crazy these days!" Brooke said all this while eyeballing Kevin's half-full plate of chicken fingers.

"I know what you mean. Jace and I are still in an apartment, too, but...unless he's been hiding a secret account from me, we haven't really been working on saving up."

Jace shrugged, and a smile tugged at the corner of his mouth.

"Are you guys going to get married someday?" Brooke blurted.

Kennedy found the question off-putting and too personal. *Maybe we couldn't be friends after all...*

"W-we, um, well..." Kennedy stuttered. She shook her leg up and down like a hot piston.

"It's not out of the realm of possibilities," Jace stated, resting his palm over Kennedy's neatly folded fingers planted on the table. He did this from time to time to calm her nerves. She stopped shaking her leg the instant his cool hand pressed against hers.

"Ah, well, good luck with that. Gosh, I'm stuffed!" Brooke leaned back in her chair. She sucked at her teeth, running a tongue over them and bulging out her upper lip. She poked at the tab sitting on the table. Kennedy wondered if her change in direction was intentional or just aloofness woven into her social programming.

"We're going to the convenience store across the street. Need anything?" Kevin asked.

"Nah, we're good. Thanks. We're just waiting to hear about my car," Jace said.

"Okay, well, maybe we'll run into you sometime. If you go to the fair, come find us." Kevin slapped some cash on the table and tucked it under the glass saltshaker.

"It was great to meet you!" Brooke smiled. She rose from her seat as if she were pregnant, holding her side. "Food baby," she said, winking at Kennedy.

Kennedy watched the couple leave and sighed. "Can you believe she asked us that?"

"Eh, she's probably just blunt and oblivious."

"Still annoying, though.

"Maybe we should check out the fair after all."

Kennedy didn't care to see anything at the fair. What else was there to do in this town?

"What if it's lame?"

"If it's lame, we can laugh at it. Besides, we can find Kevin and Brooke and hang out with them."

"Hopefully, she'll chill out on the third-degree questions."

They sat at the café for a while longer, procrastinating while watching patrons come and go. That young waitress, Adrienne, sat at a table with another girl. As the diner grew quieter, she eavesdropped on Adrienne chastising her.

"You din' put it on right. Now yer burnt," she said. The girl rubbed her arm, and Kennedy saw there wasn't just a burn but flesh peeling from a swipe on her shoulder with yellow bubbles dotting the perimeter. Adrienne shot a glance at Kennedy, who jerked her head back to Jace. Sweat prickled at her forehead, and the baby hairs poked out from the back of her neck.

"Let's get out of here," she said.

5

Trashy Ride

"Think we can hoof it?" Jace stepped onto the dusty white parking lot and squinted at the afternoon sun.

Kennedy shaded her eyes and saw a hint of a carnival ride in the hazy distance. "Yeah, it doesn't look that far. I can make out the top of one of the rides."

"All right, let's walk then. Probably don't need this map." Jace pressed his hand against his pocket, crushing the chicken scratch map under the fabric.

They had only made it several feet down the road when the sound of crunching tires came to a halt next to them.

"Hey, guys! Did you decide to go to the fair?" Kevin and Brooke peered at them from the open window of their late-model Honda. They looked like two cockatoos tilting their heads to the side.

"Yeah, you got room?" Kennedy asked. Despite being put off by Brooke, she was glad they hadn't left yet.

"Get in!" Kevin pressed the door lock and got out to open the back door for Kennedy. She slid in behind Brooke on the passenger side, and Jace sat behind Kevin.

Their car was a disaster. Empty cans littered the floor—some crushed and some still in their cylindrical form, dribbling old syrupy soda. There was an odd funk in the cabin interior that was a mixture of squirrel hair caught in the radiator and fast food that had permeated the fabric. Kennedy made a face at Jace, who just smiled and shook his head.

"Glad we caught you!" Kevin turned around and grinned with a complete perfect set of white teeth.

"Yeah, me too. We most likely would have regretted walking the whole way." As Kennedy buckled her belt, her thumb pressed into a congealed blob of ketchup on the button release. She held her breath and her tongue, sitting about a half inch above the seat and hoping her disgust didn't show.

"We should totally go to the demo derby!" Brooke flailed her hands.

"I really don't know about that." Kennedy disagreed with the couple's ideas of fun. The few interactions she'd had with the townies had already put her on edge, and the constant undercurrent of banjo music gave her a headache.

"I'll give you my number...just because. That way, we can keep in touch when we get home." Brooke scrawled her number on a crumpled gas receipt from the center console and handed it to Kennedy. The heat-printed paper was faded, but Kennedy could make out the date as being from last year. She wondered how someone who made a living in a clean room could stand to see so much trash piled in her car. She pocketed the number but didn't attempt to find another scrap of paper to return the favor.

Between wrangling the seatbelt and scribbling down the phone number, it didn't take long to reach the fair. The parking lot was a large swath of grass, and it was packed. Kevin drove slowly over the lawn, bumping over deep tire tracks.

"Ah, here's a spot," he said, turning into a skinny space between a large blue truck with rust on the rims and a smaller red truck with silver balls swinging from the hitch and a peeling bumper sticker that said, "My Other Car Is a Motorcycle." Kennedy rolled her eyes and chuffed.

The four got out of the car, and Brooke stretched her arms high, growling and smacking her lips. Half the people meandering toward the fair chatted to one another in twang. The other half, Kennedy noticed, appeared to be outsiders like them. She relaxed a little, knowing she wouldn't be completely surrounded by townies and, even worse, carnies. The warm smell of funnel cakes and popcorn wafted through the breeze, along with the nagging scent of sunscreen. Kennedy pinched the bridge of her nose, stifling a swelling sneeze and a migraine.

"I still have room," Brooke said, patting her stomach.

"I assume you're talking about the fair food and not guzzling a bottle of sunscreen." Kennedy squeezed her eyes shut, rubbing her face pink.

"What? Sunscreen?" Brooke sniffed the air. "Oh, I guess I kinda smell that."

Kinda? The air was swollen with the metallic smell of titanium dioxide and zinc; Kennedy wanted to take a shower.

Spinning colors and rides came into focus as they headed toward the din of shouts and more banjo music. Kennedy was sickened by the smell of cigarette smoke mingled with fresh popcorn and lemonade shakers over the heavy SPF. Several kids ran back and forth, screaming and laughing as their slow parents shouted at them with colorful cursing. One particular mom waddled toward her twin toddlers with her pregnant belly protruding so far beyond her knees that she looked like she could pop at any moment.

"Well, this looks like it could be *the* event of the year in this town," Kevin said.

"Yeah, they wouldn't stop talking about it at the café before you showed up," Kennedy rolled her eyes and wondered if she'd see those two men from the diner.

"Four, please," Brooke said to the ticket attendant.

"Oh, you don't have to buy our tickets!" Kennedy frowned.

"It's no problem at all! Besides, I'm so happy we met you guys. These things are so much more fun with friends." Brooke pulled out her wallet and shuffled through leaves of bills. Kennedy watched her and thought about that. *Friends.* She was never good at meeting people or keeping them around. Friends were hard. Friends were *work*. Only Jace made a relationship easy. That is, when he wasn't neglecting basic car maintenance. She felt the crinkle in her pocket where Brooke's number sat on the old crusty receipt and wondered how much work this friendship might be. She dreaded the thought of constant text exchanges and the obligation to reply every time Brooke had a thought in her head. Was she that kind of person?

Kennedy didn't realize she was looking at her feet until the image of a cheap pull-tab ticket was thrust into her view, grasped at the edge by Brooke's thumb and forefinger; Brooke waved it a little to get her attention. Kennedy only noticed a fingernail chipped in the corner with a small piece of blue fuzz clinging to the jagged edge.

"Thanks. I appreciate it." Kennedy took the ticket and pasted on a fake grin, shuddering inside at Brooke's simplistic hygiene.

They wandered into the fairgrounds, taking in the sights and sounds of the carnival rides, as well as the shouts of wild children and equally wild parents. Puffs of cotton candy bobbed around as the owners strolled with them in hand. There was even a clown not far from the entrance entertaining children with his balloon animals. Kennedy hated clowns.

She didn't know what she wanted to do first...ride something that was probably held together with duct tape and chewing gum or just delight in the greasy fair menu. She looked at her phone for any sign of life.

She turned to Jace and poked his shoulder. "Do you have a signal yet?"

He opened his phone and didn't see any bars but noticed a voice-mail icon at the top. He tried to listen to it, but the message wouldn't load. "I can't listen to it, but I'm willing to bet it's Gearhead," he said.

"So we can leave tomorrow?"

"Well, I don't know. I can't hear the message. Maybe we can stop by the auto shop after hanging out here for a while."

Kennedy thought about that for a moment. She wanted nothing more than the guarantee that she would be out of this town first thing in the morning. She also didn't want to walk all the way back to Douglas Auto, only on Jace's hunch. "Okay, we'll stop by after."

Brooke leaned over and interrupted, "Hey, did I hear your car is fixed? We should celebrate by going to the demo derby!"

Kennedy grimaced. "All right, all right, we'll go to the stupid demo derby! And no, the car isn't fixed—at least that we know of."

A man with thick-rimmed glasses and a tipped fedora walked right in front of them, nearly stepping on Kennedy's foot.

"Excuse you!" she shouted as he strolled away. He waved his hand dismissively and continued deeper into the fray. He wore a striped shirt that made him look like Waldo. "So rude!"

"Yeah, this place attracts many folks from the city for some reason," Kevin said. "You'll see a bunch of snobby pricks wandering around trying to get a taste of 'country life'... I personally think it's their way of flaunting their so-called higher status to a bunch of rednecks."

"Wow, that was profound," Kennedy said, laughing. She scanned the field to see several city people. It was a sea of trucker hats and overalls mingled with Dockers and man buns.

"Maybe they're just trying to have fun, Kev." Brooke poked him, and he shrugged.

As they talked, a swarm of people surrounded them, funneling their way toward the opposite side of the fair. They turned their attention to the direction of the crowd and noticed a colorful arena filling up with bodies.

"Oh, would you look at that? The demo derby is right *now!*" Brooke clapped as she nodded toward the arena.

Kennedy wasn't ready for this. After slumping her shoulders and taking a deep breath, she glanced at a smaller booth with a short line that had a painted image of chips in a basket. "I want to get some nachos first," she said.

6

The Derb

Jace and Kennedy found some seats high in the wooden bleachers and set their nachos into two empty spots near them for Kevin and Brooke. After Kennedy had mentioned nachos, Brooke was struck with a craving for funnel cake and dragged Kevin away to another small booth with a similar painted sign. Unlike the basket of nachos, the funnel cake sign looked like a coiled turd.

"Man, I didn't even get to ride anything," Jace said. He pouted as he plopped down into the seat.

"Maybe afterward. If we have time."

The sunscreen smell was back, hanging over the arena like a heavy cloud of plastic coconut perfume. The arena was packed, with rows and rows of people in varying degrees of sophistication. Half the stands were filled with outsiders, wearing "city" clothes in a variety of styles. The other half undulated in excitement—some with exposed tender pink flesh reddened by the sun, others donning their usual torn tees with or without overalls. Kennedy saw a few of these people barefoot and muddy, cursing like sailors with their children clinging to them wearing dirt mustaches. A gang of hollering teenage boys near the front row swung blankets around, shouting through cigarettes clamped between brown teeth.

The hollow thud of a spotlight echoed, illuminating the already sunny arena. The cheers swelled. Kennedy saw the large pregnant woman with her toddlers across the way in the front, fumbling with some drink she assumed was spilling because the woman's mouth kept opening and closing in the shape of curses. She scanned over to the right of the pregnant woman and saw two other women who happened to lock eyes with her at the same time. She looked at Jace, who was smiling at the crowd, and then she turned back to the women again. They were still staring right at her. Kennedy waved at them for some confirmation, and they turned away. Kennedy shivered.

Jace put his arm around her. "You okay?"

Her eyes remained fixed on the strange duo who had found interest in a different couple closer to them. "Y-yeah, I think I'm just a little cold."

"Cold? Really? In this heat?"

"You're a man. You run hot."

"I know that, but it's like *afternoon*. In the middle of summer." Jace tightened his grip around her shoulder, pulling her closer to him. She felt the heat radiating from his side, which gave her some comfort from the chilly stares.

"We're back!" Brooke almost sat on Kennedy's tray of nachos before springing back up like cold water hitting her back. "Oops! sorry!" Once the nachos were safely in Kennedy's grip, Brooke plopped down onto the bench with the plate of sugar-dusted funnel cake on her lap. She rubbed her hands together.

"You cold?" she asked, catching Kennedy jammed under Jace's armpit.

Kennedy nodded, then swiveled her head up at Jace, who was already deep in conversation with Kevin. She turned her attention back to Brooke, who was staring at the arena, stuffing chunks of funnel cake in her mouth with an aloofness about her.

Kennedy cleared her throat. "Hey, have you noticed anything..." She looked back toward the odd women, who were staring back again.

"...weird around here?" She kept her voice low; afraid speaking would catch on the breeze and deliver her message directly into their ears.

"Weird? What do you mean?" Brooke continued to pop the cake in her mouth. The blue fuzz was still clinging to her jagged fingernail.

"Don't look, but...there's a pair of women across the way just...s taring at us."

"They're staring at us?" Brooke rolled her eyes sideways in the direction of the women. She at least knew how to look inconspicuous. Her jaw flexed, and her eyes widened. "What's their *problem*?" she whispered through the spongy cake, blowing the scent of fried sugar into Kennedy's nose.

"I don't know. They give me the heebies," Kennedy whispered back, trying not to make eye contact with them.

She noticed that a few seats away from her on the same bench was the man in the red hat who had helped them on the side of the road earlier. She gave him a meek wave that Brooke noticed. Unlike the unnerving pair of women across the track, Red Hat smiled and waved back. He mouthed something Kennedy couldn't make out, so she put a hand to her ear and mouthed to him that she couldn't hear him.

Red Hat rocked back and rose on stumpy legs, pushing down on his right knee to help himself up. He hobbled toward her, dodging the knees and feet of other guests. His meaty butt cheek bumped the head of a pony-tailed brunette in the row in front of them. She rocked forward and rubbed her head, her mouth twisting into an *O* as her sister rubbed her back.

"Hey there! Did yeh get yer car taken care of?" He squeezed himself next to Brooke and the small boy who sat next to her. The boy glared at him.

"Well, we talked to Gearhead. And we're hoping it'll be done by tomorrow."

"Good deal." He tipped the bill of his hat, similar to the way she'd seen several others do throughout the day. He also smelled like sunscreen and beer. Kennedy was sick and tired of the thick scent of Coppertone and redneck sweat.

Their conversation was interrupted by the high-pitched wail of microphone feedback. Everyone groaned in unison, then laughed and turned their attention to the front of the arena. "Welp, better get back to my seat!" Red Hat left almost as soon as he sat down.

A scrawny man with big eyes shouted at the crowd. "Everyone, please welcome our highly talented demo derby judge and announcer...our very own sheriff!"

A different man resembling a skeleton in a skin suit stepped up onto the covered podium. A tall, tan trucker cap smashed down his pouf of brownish-red curly hair. A slender cigarette poked between his lips, and he tapped on the microphone again, making it squeal in protest.

"I guess it's on," he muttered, then laughed into it. He didn't look like a sheriff to Kennedy.

A swell of cheers erupted on the townie half of the stands. Kennedy saw the fedora man and his smug mug, peering around with his arms folded.

"Ladieeees and gents!" the skinny man shouted as the loudspeaker wailed. "Welcome teh Royal Lake's second annual demo derby!" His voice popped into the microphone and changed in pitch, making Kennedy feel like she was riding one of the roller coasters.

The crowd cheered and whistled. The townie near Kennedy shouted so loud she felt the bones in her ear vibrate. A chipped yellow junker with the bold number one painted on the side buzzed onto the field, followed by several other vehicles in varying states of decay. They drove in an arc around the arena as the announcer continued.

"Leadin' the pack at number one is Colllllby's Cruuuusherrrr!" the sheriff shouted, clamping the cigarette between his lips as if he couldn't bear to part with it. "An' behind the wheel is'r guest driver from Springfield, Pete Parsons! Give it up fer Pete!"

The crowd roared as the yellow car with the number one bounced over the hills in the dirt, spinning circles and sending waves of dust from the tires.

"This is what people do for fun?" Kennedy whispered to Jace, who laughed.

"Oh, come on. This beats Tool any day, babe!" His sarcasm was thick.

A blue car introduced as the Gambit had the number four painted on its side and also spun around, showing off its moves. The sheriff continued to introduce each vehicle and their drivers. According to the list, Kennedy caught that most of the drivers were townies, but a couple of drivers were guests from the city.

"Well, with all things considered, this has been an interesting journey," she said.

"And I'm glad to be here with you," Jace's wide smile shrunk down into a straight line. "About that marriage thing..."

"Don't." Kennedy shot a look at Brooke, who was happily ignoring them and watching the cars bang into one another. Peering back at Jace, she whispered, "She was just being intrusive and probably didn't mean anything by it. Please don't give it another thought. I'm happy!"

"Are you?"

"Of course I am. We're young, right? We have *so* much time." She felt Jace eyeing her. "Look, I'm not opposed to marriage, but if you're not ready to do that, I'm okay with it."

He paused, gazing directly at her, his elbow propped on a bent knee in his thinker pose. "What makes you think I'm not ready?"

Kennedy opened her mouth, but a bang and crunch followed by screams and gasps broke into their conversation. They jerked their heads toward the arena.

Colby's Crusher was pressed against the barrier, its tires spinning a few inches above the ground as if the driver thought he could create enough speed to fly up and away. He was pinned. The sound of collapsing metal from the driver's-side door rang out like nails on a chalkboard as the Gambit's tires smoked in perpetual reversal. *Ping! Ping! Ping!* Each dent cried out as the yellow number one became smaller and smaller, resembling a wad of tin foil crumpled into a ball.

Kennedy sprang up like a jackrabbit, and others followed her. Jace grabbed her hand. She saw that the driver of the Gambit knew what he was doing. Yellow and blue were the closest cars to them. Others dotted the arena with their own victims trapped against the barrier. The symphony of screeching tires crescendoed, and Kennedy heard several pleas for them to stop. "What are you doing? The driver is going to die! Someone do something!" Some outsiders were even petitioning the sheriff to intervene, but he just stood there leaning against the podium rail, taking lazy drags from his cigarette.

Colby's Crusher folded in on itself. Kennedy jumped as its engine burst into flames. Another pinned car's engine popped, followed by two more. Townies cheered, and outsiders screamed. The final crush had completely flattened Colby's Crusher, and she knew Dan Parsons was dead.

Kennedy froze. Then the strangest thing happened: the arena went silent. A trickle of blood spilled from the driver's-side door.

One by one, the townies panted. Their chests quickened as though they were possessed. The panting was a rhythmic wave that pulsed through the arena.

Hoo-hah hoo-hah hoo-hah.

The crackle of flames and the whoosh of a fire extinguisher from an arena worker added background ambiance, and Kennedy's ears swelled with the pounding of her blood.

The townies rushed the arena, scattering among the destroyed vehicles, undulating In a wave of intensity, clawing at one another and screaming. With open mouths, they clamored and raged toward the bloody stream. The pregnant woman she'd seen earlier hungrily licked her fingers as she repeatedly dunked them into the stream. Her small children clutched at her ankles, their little open maws catching the dribbles of red from their mother's hand. The skinny man Kennedy recognized from the diner opened the driver's-side door and dragged out the body.

The panicked screams of all the outsiders broke the silence. The wooden bleachers creaked and groaned as the stampede roared from the arena. Kennedy remained frozen, Jace's heat radiating next to her as they stood arm to arm. One particularly harried spectator bumped into her elbow.

The driver was flat and broken in so many places. Limbs stuck out at odd angles while the townies bobbed over and around him. Kennedy didn't know how long she stood there, watching a small child fill her sippy cup with thick, warm red Kool-Aid. Jace squeezed her arm and tugged at it. It was a gentle tug for whatever reason. Maybe she was dreaming?

Brooke let out a quivering cry, and Kevin had gone white—he stood slack with his mouth open and eyes vacant. This definitely was not a dream.

Kennedy grabbed Brooke's shoulders and shook her. "We *have* to get out of here!" Her voice vibrated, and she felt her hands go cold as fight-or-flight kicked in.

She yanked on Jace's hand, and they stuttered down the stairs to make their escape. The scene blurred by as they ran.

The remaining outsiders scattered like cockroaches as the pile of hungry hillbillies feasted on the driver. As an eerie orange glow flickered across the pile of townies, Kennedy realized the opposite side of the arena had caught fire.

7

Fire, Fire

"Fire! It's always gotta be fire!" Birdseed spat on the ground, flicking another cigarette from the box and wet-lipping the end.

A scared teen with a collared blue-striped shirt darted from behind the stands, holding a stick on fire. Birdseed watched him go with one elbow leaning on the rail of the podium and the other hand scratching his chin.

The kid whimpered with each strike of the foot as he marathoned through the mess of panicked outsiders, carrying his fiery beacon. Chuckling, Birdseed surveyed the area for Wyatt. He found him standing down by one of the drivers, cursing at the other townies.

Looking up at Birdseed, he shouted, "He's all dry. I din't get none!"

Birdseed sighed, rolled his eyes, and sarcastically pointed at the scattering crowd.

8

SHED TOOLS

KENNEDY'S FEET HIT THE ground, but she didn't feel it. Jace ran beside her with Brooke and Kevin trailing. Flames licked the edges of her peripheral vision. Brooke's panting struck her ears over and over among the screams of others around them. Her breathing morphed into the sound of the townies' bloodlust.

Hoo-hah-hoo-hah-hoo-hah.

"We have to get to the car!" She wasn't sure if they heard her, but her veering toward the lawn parking lot gave them the cue they needed to follow.

They passed the nacho stand, where one hillbilly managed to wrangle the city jerk with the fedora. Kennedy had to take a second look because she swore the guy's knees were banging against the fedora guy's skull. Was he perched on the guy's shoulders? His trendy specs flew from his face.

"Whee! Look, son! 'Es a buckin' bronco!"

Fedora windmilled his arms around, feebly slapping at the monkey on his back. The gangly creature giggled and made lasso motions with his arm. A puff of red mist burst from the guy's neck, and his knees went slack. Kennedy nearly slammed into Jace when he screeched to a halt in the middle of the field.

Others zigzagged across the field. As they stood there, Kennedy heard the faint sound of fair music with the spin of the Ferris wheel.

Are they still running rides? She glanced over her shoulder to see a co-ordinated gallop of bare feet and overalls. *We're sitting ducks out in the open!*

"Jace, what are you *doing*?" she cried.

"Look!" He pointed toward the ticket booths.

"Are you kidding me?" Kevin said. "This whole *town* is insane!"

The silhouettes of each booth attendant stepped out of their enclosures to face them in a game of chicken. The sound of pounding feet in the grass loomed closer and closer.

Hoo-hah-hoo-hah-hoo-hah!

"Damn!" Kennedy dug her heels into the grass and grabbed Jace's arm before tugging him toward the surrounding woods. Other outsiders also disappeared into the trees. Brooke and Kevin were at their heels, not making a peep other than their heavy breathing.

Several paces later, the woods had swallowed them, with the sounds of other outsiders rushing through the brush and whimpering. A strange thought hit Kennedy: how many children were in this fray? How many children were a *part* of the fray?

She thought about that pregnant woman, greedily slurping up Dan's insides like a rabid dog, ready to give birth to her baby hyena. The children standing by her side only followed what Mommy did. What kind of town was this?

Kennedy spotted a shed on the side of an outhouse with peeling white paint and a caved-in roof.

"There!" she said, pointing. The other three followed her without question.

Maybe they could hide here. Maybe there were weapons in here. Either way, it was something.

"What are we going to find in there?" Brooke asked, her voice trembling.

Kennedy strutted toward the shed door and kicked it open.

"Nice," Jace said, jogging up to the structure with her. He poked his head inside.

The thick, earthy scent of mildew nearly shut down Kennedy's lungs and made her gasp. "There's got to be something in here," she said, pulling her shirt over her nose and mouth.

The shed was only big enough for two people. Kevin and Brooke stood by, anxiously darting their heads left and right for signs of other outsiders and crazies.

"Here..." Kennedy stuck her hand out as she held an old plastic rake to Brooke.

"What am I going to do with this?" she whined.

"It's better than nothing, hon. Just take it." Kevin grabbed the rake and made her wrap her fingers around the handle.

"The only other thing in here is a shovel." Jace clamped onto the shovel and poked the end into the dirt as though it were a magic staff.

"I have my belt!" Kennedy undid her pleather belt and wrapped a portion around her fist, letting the sharp buckle dangle.

"Oh, I have keys!" Kevin laced his car key, house key, and gate key between his knuckles.

"Okay, we're all armed now," Kennedy said, "but it's best if we don't engage at all."

The forest shuddered next to them, and Gearhead emerged from a thick parcel of trees.

"Oh, heya. Di' yeh get mah *message*?"

Kennedy spun around, and her buckle slapped against her thigh. Jace double-fisted the shovel, and Brooke scampered behind him with her rake. Kevin stood in front, looking down at his knuckles. He shrugged and thrust his fist forward, pointy sides out while guarding his face with the other arm.

"I saw you *left* a message, but I didn't have a chance to hear it," Jace said, gripping the handle tighter.

Gearhead smirked. "All I said is, seems I don' need ta order them parts." He took a few steps toward them. "But I reckon yeh won' be needin' yer car."

Kennedy sniffed the air. It was that cursed sunscreen again. She couldn't help it; she had to sneeze.

She blew out her sneeze, nearly whipping herself in the head with her buckle. Brooke jumped. Kevin hit himself in the face. Jace swung his shovel, connecting with Gearhead's ear.

The metal clanged like a gong, and Gearhead fell to the ground. "Ow!" he said, putting a fat hand against his head.

"Run!" Jace pointed toward the parking lot.

They sprinted through the thicket, making their way toward the back of the lot, out of sight of the ticket attendants.

9

THE TICKET MASTERS

"DID YEH GET ANY?" Birdseed huffed as he caught up to Wyatt in the open field. They strolled past the Ferris wheel, where the carnival operator was slumped over the controls with several punctures. He looked dry.

"Nah. Still outta shape. Prob'ly worse now, I think." Wyatt rubbed his concave belly.

"Here, have a lil of this." Birdseed unscrewed a Mason jar and handed it to Wyatt.

"Really? Yeh mean it? Di' yeh have some too?"

"Yeah, I'm good."

"Thanks, man." Wyatt took an oversized swig of the contents. "Which driver yeh get this from?"

"Ol' Danny. He was a good'un, and I was sorry ta see 'im go, but well...we gotta eat."

"I ken already feel mah strength comin' back."

"Strength or no, I ain't turnin' into no bat again." Birdseed spat on the ground.

Wyatt nodded, kicking at the grass. "Hey, 'seed?"

"Yeah?"

"D'ya think we got Big Greasy's curse?"

"Well, duh, seems like."

"I know tha' much, but I mean, are we damned? 's God mad a'us?"

Birdseed adjusted the bill of his hat. He chewed around on a cigarette before lighting it up and taking a pensive drag. "We din' make tha' deal."

Wyatt knew this. He'd read Big Greasy's journal a thousand times, hoping something in his descent into madness would be a clue to their redemption. But he never found it.

"Nah we din'," he said, "but we's murderers now."

A faint carnival tune droned in the distance.

"Would God punish us fer som'thin' we can't control?" asked Birdseed.

"We were suppos'ta protect 'n' serve. Not curse 'em all and kill our guests. Big Greasy lived for cen'tries on squirrel and 'coons."

"Well, what yeh wanna do 'bout it now, Wy?"

"We ken jes die. Or we should'a jes let ourselves die."

Birdseed shrugged and looked up at the sky. "Maybe."

Wyatt paused for a long minute. "Hey 'seed?"

"Yeah?"

"Do yeh think God'll fergive me?"

Birdseed chuckled and clapped him on the shoulder. "Of course he will."

"What about Adrienne?"

"I hope so, bud. I dunno, tho'. She's helpin' us a bit by keepin' the strangers here in town."

"How's she doin' that?"

"She's got her ways."

Wyatt sighed again. He tormented himself over the affliction that was passed to him from the Devil. He was cursed, and he was afraid it made him unclean to God. But he wondered if Birdseed had a point. They couldn't control what had happened to them. They couldn't control the spread to the rest of the town since they didn't know what they were doing. He couldn't control his thirst. He resolved to worry about it another day—it was hunting season now.

"Heads-up," Birdseed said, pointing.

A couple of stragglers hobbled by, making their way toward the ticket booths. One of them had a twisted ankle, and he limped in double time.

"Hey, watch this," Wyatt said. He made exaggerated tiptoeing marches through the grass. He then leapt in the air, aiming for the shoulders of the injured stranger, but he made the mistake of spreading all his limbs outward like a flying squirrel. The wounded man spun around, along with his friend, and saw Wyatt spread-eagled in the air, attempting a belly-flop onto their heads. They ducked to the side, sending Wyatt sprawling in the grass. The group audibly shuddered and picked up speed toward the ticket booths.

"Still clumsy, though," Birdseed said, chuckling as he jogged up to Wyatt, who lay prone on the ground. He offered his hand to get his friend to his feet, then patted his shoulder. "Don' worry. Yeh'll get it right someday. Plus, the ticket masters'll get 'em."

"They'd better got jars with 'em. Ol' John-Po's a pig. He'll suck 'em dry 'fore savin' any."

10

Sweeter than Sweet Tea

As Jace and Kennedy approached the lot, they slowed down, with Kevin and Brooke following close behind. Brooke held her rake so tightly that she might break it or twist hundreds of rotted wood splinters into her palm.

Kennedy scanned the lot for signs of the ticket masters. They were far enough away from the booths that they could safely sneak through the rows of cars. After reaching Brooke and Kevin's car, she saw them.

The ticket masters had their backs to the group. She counted five...six of them. They seemed preoccupied with something, so she ducked down and motioned for the others to do the same. Kevin unlocked the door, and they all crawled inside.

Brooke shut her door and bit down on her knuckle. "Oh, my God!. Oh, my God!" She screamed into her hand. Kennedy was shocked at how Brooke was unraveling.

"Dude, I think these townies are like...vampires or something!" Kevin hissed.

"No way! It's the middle of the day... Wouldn't they die in the sun? And aren't vampires supposed to be all sexy and stuff? They're hillbillies!" Kennedy cried.

"Wait, I thought they were rednecks." Jace tapped his lip.

"What the hell's the difference?" Brooke cried.

"Dude, watch where you're pointing that thing," Kevin said, shifting away from Brooke's plastic rake prongs.

"All right, let's calm down," Kennedy blew out a heavy breath and squeezed the belt coil around her hand. "Can we just get out of here, please?"

Kevin nodded and shook as he tried to unwind the keys from between his knuckles. They left deep impressions in his flesh. He slid the key into the ignition and twisted it. *Click, click, click!* Nothing.

"What the hell?" Brooke said.

Kevin tried again. *Click, click, click!* Nothing.

"We just had the car at the dealer!" Brooke exclaimed. "Why won't it freakin' start?"

"Okay, we need to come up with a new plan," Kennedy said in a frenzy, "Aside from the sunlight, we think these guys might be vamps, right?"

"And hillbillies," Jace added.

"Whatever. Let's say they're vampires...what else are they weak against?"

Brooke bit her lower lip. "I don't know. Garlic?"

Kennedy poked her foot around at the trash in the car, hoping to find an old takeaway box that might have remnants of garlic from a pizza or burger—no such luck.

"What else?"

"Well, we could always stake them in the heart?" Jace offered.

"Yes, wonderful." Kennedy rolled her eyes. "Kevin, do you have a *stake*?"

"A stake? What kind of engineer do you think I am?" he said. "Of course I have a stake."

He pulled a short, sharpened piece of wood from the floorboard of the passenger seat. He waggled it back and forth, making Jace laugh. Kevin shrugged.

"I-I like to LARP," he said.

Kennedy raised an eyebrow. "LARP?"

"You know...live-action role play?"

"What kind of live-action games are you playing?" Jace said, laughing again and swiping the stake.

"Uh-uh, fun ones...interesting ones. Like..." He lowered his voice. "*Vampire: the Masquerade.*"

Kennedy snorted.

"How did I not know that about you?" Brooke said in a huff. They all burst out laughing.

A stone crashed through the windshield, bouncing off the center console and hitting Jace's chest.

The young brunette waitress, Adrienne, stood in front of their hood, holding out a glass pitcher of light-brown liquid. Jace gripped the stake harder, and they all froze in place.

"Hey, y'all thirsty? I got some sweet tea here if youn's want some! Me an' my frien's thought yer car might get thirsty too, so we made sure to pour a nice heaping gallon into each gas tank here in this lot." She threw back her head and cackled.

"Crap!" Kennedy muttered.

"I knew it!" Brooke cursed.

"We have to get out of the car and away from her. On three..." Kennedy nodded at each of them.

"One..."

Kevin slid his fingers through the door handle.

"Two..."

Brooke and Jace put one hand on the door and another over the slim chrome lever.

"Three!"

Kennedy burst from the car. Before she could say or do anything, Jace rushed toward Adrienne with the LARP stake in hand.

She hissed at him, baring a wide row of pointed teeth. She wasn't able to fight back at the surprise attack, though. The pointed end of the stake sank directly through her ribs, landing wetly into her heart.

Jace pulled his hand away, shaking. Adrienne dropped her pitcher of tea. It shattered in the grass, and she wobbled on the spot.

"Wut...did yeh d-do," she grumbled. The tips of her fingers felt around the blunt end of the stake protruding from her torso, and a trickle of blood leaked from the corner of her mouth.

Was she human, after all? Kennedy took quick breaths, nearly passing out from hyperventilation.

"I'm sorry! I'm sorry!" Jace stammered. He backed away with his hands to his mouth.

"I...I was j-jus—" Her body burst into a cone of gore, flinging bits of rotting organs at the group.

Brooke screamed as fleshy shrapnel peppered Kennedy. The pieces smelled like sunscreen and iron. "Euagh!" She shivered, shook the chunks from her clothes, and used her shoulder to wipe her chin.

"Okay, I guess there's a bit of a...delay," Kevin said. He strode over to the blast circle and snatched the stake that had fallen into the grass. "But it seems like one bit of vampire lore still works on this breed."

"Guys, we need to get out of sight and make a new plan," With the hem of her shirt, Kennedy wiped the red from her forearm. She peered down at her shoe and saw Adrienne's low bun disconnected and resting on her foot. She shuddered and kicked it like a hacky sack.

"We're going back where we came from." Jace pointed to the treeline.

Kevin and Brooke didn't argue. Brooke snatched up the rake, and Kevin held his LARP stake out as if he were handing over a bouquet, pointy end first. They crouch-ran toward the trees and disappeared into the woods.

They regrouped at the shed, for one, hoping to unearth any other useful tool and, for two, to digest what they'd just seen.

"Gearhead is gone," Kennedy whispered. They all peered at the patch of grass where they'd left him, now vacant.

"You didn't hit him hard enough," Brooke said, gripping her rake and twisting her fists around the handle again. She wrinkled her nose at Jace.

They heard noises rustling in bushes all over the forest and a few whispers. Several outsiders had taken refuge within the trees.

"Psst!" a voice hissed from a nearby shrub. Jace spun around, looking for the noise. "Over here!" the voice whispered. The top of a black trucker hat peeped over the bush, and Kennedy stumbled back.

"He's one of them, guys! Look at the hat!"

"One a' who? One a' *them*?" The man stood from his hiding spot, jabbing a finger in the direction of the demo derby. He had a collared red flannel shirt buttoned up and tucked into tight jeans. His cowboy boots had such a curl at the toe that an elf would be jealous.

Brooke choked. "What is *wrong* with you hillbillies?"

"Hillbillies?" The man stepped closer to the group. They backed away in unison. "I ain't no damn hillbilly! I'm what you'd call...a *redneck*."

He spat on the ground, then shifted the chaw around in his cheek.

"Damn right you are," another voice said from the shed.

Gearhead.

He leapt on the guy's shoulders, turning his redneck into an actual red neck. Kennedy let out a weird noise like she was trying to blow out a candle while doing crunches at the gym. Brooke bolted.

"Brooke!" Kevin ran after her.

"Run, Kay!" Jace shouted as Kennedy stood there, slack-jawed at watching the stranger being tapped like a keg. She didn't know when Jace had told her to run, but when it hit her ears, she ran.

The only place she knew to go was deeper into the woods. After a few seconds, she heard another *thonk!* then "Ow!"

Jace must have bonked Gearhead's bean again with the shovel. She hoped he got away.

11

Cone of Silence

Birdseed poked the man with the twisted ankle with his toe. He rolled over, wearing a sheet-white face.

"Empty," he told Wyatt, who stood eagerly holding his Mason jar.

"Wut about the friend?" he asked.

"He's dry, too."

Wyatt glared at the ticket masters. All four of them leaned against their booths, picking at their teeth. "Yer all hogs, tha lot of ya!"

The man on the end casually gave Wyatt the finger and then continued to pick his teeth.

Wyatt sighed and held his stomach. "Still don' really know wut I'm doin' with this new huntin' thing. I jes do wut I can. Sorry, man."

"Don't worry," said Birdseed. "We'll get more. Jus' be glad we ken at least save jars for a year."

"I hate blood jelly," Wyatt groaned.

"Wanna make ice cream?"

Wyatt perked up, cracking a smile.

"I thought yeh'd like that." Birdseed clapped Wyatt's shoulder and guided him toward the parking lot.

"Maybe we could pickle it somehow...or yeh know what? I bet we ken make some fruit leather from it!" Wyatt talked like an excited boy, coming up with new ideas for preserving their annual hunt.

"Hm, blood leather. Tha' might be good too. Last us a year, I reckon."

"Yeah! An' we ken gather all the town's jars, and—"

Birdseed jerked his arm in front of Wyatt and sniffed the air; it had a foul smell.

The buzz of flies and gnats vibrated in his ear. The noises gained pitch as he and Wyatt moved deeper into the parking lot.

A circle of red radiated outward in the grass, forming an arc near a cluster of vehicles.

Wyatt cocked his head to the side. "Wut's that?"

They tiptoed toward the painted cone, with Birdseed rising farther on his toes as they got closer.

"Wut *is* that?" Wyatt bent down and picked up a squishy brown ball. He held it in front of Birdseed, who'd already found tattered clothes scattered around a broken tea pitcher. *Adrienne.*

His lower lip quivered. He snatched the ball from Wyatt and held it to his nose, taking in a deep breath.

"Adrienne! Adrienne!" he shouted. The faraway shadows of the ticket masters turned their way.

Wyatt backed up and grimaced. "W-wut happened to her?"

"Yeh think I know?!" Birdseed rubbed the ball of hair over his cheek and hit himself in the forehead with it. "Adrienne..." he sobbed.

Wyatt had never seen his friend like this. It was weird. "We gon' find out who did this," he said, trembling.

Birdseed's face turned down in a scowl. He reached for his pack of cigarettes, pulled one out, and stuck it in the corner of his mouth.

"Damn right we are," he said. He glanced up to the sky and cracked a wide smile. His pointy incisors hung over his lower lip as smoke trailed from the tip of his cigarette. "They can't be too far. My girl put tea 'n their tanks. Le's go."

12

IT'S JUST BROOKE

KENNEDY RAN. SHE WANTED to stay with Jace, but she ran because he'd told her to. She was alone now—no Brooke, no Kevin, no boyfriend.

She reasoned that Jace would be okay after clocking Gearhead. Deeper in the thicket, she filtered into a crowd of other fairgoers also funneling deeper inside. She passed a larger woman with a Rorschach sweat stain spreading on her back and a strong aroma of beer. She was wheezing and limping while wiping away the wet, stringy hair clinging to her forehead. The whoops and hollers of hillbillies echoed behind them.

"I see 'em! I see 'em! Look at 'em run!"

More whooping.

Kennedy slowed to a jog next to the struggling woman. "Are you okay?" she asked.

With a sharp exhale and choke, the woman nodded and eyeballed Kennedy. Her eyes were bloodshot and sagging, and her cheeks had a gray pallor. By the color of her skin, Kennedy wondered if this woman had any blood in her at all.

"There they is! Go, boy! *Go!*"

Other stragglers shot off in different directions. The woman whipped her head around, the extra skin under her jaw flapping and shaking with fear. She gripped Kennedy's wrist.

"Ow! Let go!"

With the biggest shove the woman could muster, Kennedy found herself tumbling to the ground, turning an ankle. The last thing she saw was about two inches of the woman's crack wobbling away.

"Jackass!" Kennedy scrambled backward through the pine needles and leaves toward a clip of unruly bushes. Just as she settled into her flimsy hiding spot, a handful hillbillies jogged by. She recognized both men from the diner, along with the announcer sheriff and Gear-head. She couldn't see the faces of the other two. They easily caught up to the drunk chubby woman. A void in the bush made a good peephole for Kennedy to spy on the group and plan her next move.

She was shocked to see Red Hat in the group. He galloped toward the woman. It wasn't even an hour ago that he'd sat inches from her and Brooke in the stands.

"Ooh, time to go hoggin'," he said, slapping his knees as he skipped circles around the woman. He looked to the sheriff, who'd found a tree to lean against.

"Nah, not fer me. I gotta watch my cholesterol." The sheriff grinned and chewed on the end of his cigarette.

Red Hat surveyed the woman. She shuddered, looking every which way and making that chin flap waggle around. When she realized she wasn't going anywhere, her shoulders sagged, and she shifted her gaze to her feet. Red Hat leapfrogged onto her saggy shoulders and bit down on her neck. A crimson spurt arced through the air.

"Hey, man, don' *waste* it!" Wyatt sprinted forward.

Red Hat pogo jumped from the woman, who slumped to the ground. Her legs slapped like pasty bread dough when she fell.

"Wooo! I'm drunker than a nine-eyed billy goat!" Red Hat spun around and snatched an empty jar from one of the others.

The group scuttled toward her and created innovative ways to fill their jars.

Recoiling at the sight, Kennedy let out the tiniest involuntary chirp. She squeezed her lips with her palm, knowing she'd just messed up.

The sheriff cocked his head to the side. "Yo, someone else there?" He crept toward Kennedy's bushes. None of the others paid any attention to him as they continued to fill their jars with leftovers.

He was small and skinny enough that if she could get him alone, she might be able to take him by herself. She felt a sneeze bubbling under the surface—it was the sunscreen again. She scrunched her face and squeezed her lips and nose tighter. The sheriff's lanky shadow elongated over her spot when another shout made him stop and turn.

"Hey, y'all, gotta box fer yer jars!"

Kennedy opened her eyes again, blinking the tears away. It was the young girl with the blistered burn from the diner. She sauntered toward the crowd, cradling a large box against her belly.

The others walked toward her with their jars full of sloppy red sauce and placed them in the box, clanking them against one another. The hollow thuds of each jar made Kennedy want to puke, and she *did* wonder whether those jars were full of cholesterol. Once the girl had gathered all the vessels of the soup du jour, she turned back the way she came.

"Gotta get these on ice 'fore they get all sticky!" she shouted over her shoulder.

Another call came from the direction of the demo derby arena. "You guys gotta check it out! We got a *wild* one!"

"Aw, hell yeah!" Red Hat exclaimed.

The group dashed back toward the demo pit. Kennedy let out a long breath and wiped her nose on her shirt. Then she remembered Adrienne's juices were all over it. She shook and pulled off the shirt, exposing her camisole. She then poked her head around the bush and saw the plump woman lying there in a heap.

"Karma's a bitch," she said, then felt bad about it.

A commotion of laughter and shouts rose from the arena. Kennedy ducked low and shimmied through some tall grass. When she finally focused her eyes, she choked on her spit.

Brooke!

"Get back! Get back all of you! I have a wooden stick, and I'm not afraid to use it!" Brooke swung the old rake. She had broken the plastic tines off and was waving the splintered end in one hand and a bundle of burning sticks in the other. She stood on a plinth in the center of the arena that was still a raging fire on one end and smoldering embers on the other. Her hair whipped around like golden threads in the light of the fire as she stabbed the air with her burning sticks toward the growing, interested crowd of hillbillies.

Kennedy army-crawled her way through the tall grass, hoping to formulate a plan to get Brooke out of there, but she had no plan. She darted her head around at her surroundings for something—anything—that would help her in this fight against these weirdos. She spotted the small shed to her right. Now kicking herself for not thinking about it before, she slithered backward through her previous path to go back and get a weapon.

"You don't want me!" Brooked cried. "I'm all skin and bones...and I'm...I'm full of *garlic*!"

The group burst out laughing. Wyatt stepped forward and rocked a Mason jar side to side. "Ha! Girl, garlic's in storybooks. B'sides, I don' need yer meat—I need yer juice."

Brooke stood there on the plinth, holding her stick. Her hand quaked, and a lone tear slunk down her cheek. "Y-you don't want to do this," she said.

Wyatt circled the little blonde. At that moment, he was struck by the thought of Big Greasy's wife and daughters. His eyes grew round at the sight of her tear. "Aw, dang it, girl! Don't be cryin' *now*." He stopped circling her and threw his arms down, glancing over at Birdseed.

Birdseed made a motion toward Brooke. He clearly hadn't read Wyatt's thoughts.

He bit his lip and groaned. "Yer right, though... I don't wanna...I *gotta*." His voice croaked through dry layers of flesh in his throat. The others flapped their arms, making clucking noises. "And I ain't yellow!"

Brooke started to back away, continuing to jab the fire in front of her toward Wyatt. Red Hat stepped forward next to Wyatt. "Aw, we jes wan' a little... An' a little more for the pantry, too."

"You hillbillies get away from her!" Kevin rounded up from behind the crowd and jammed the LARP stake in Red Hat's back.

The man grunted and jerked forward, trying to claw at his back. Kevin drew the stake out, and it made a *schlup* sound, jolting Red Hat upright.

"Now listen here, you—" Red Hat started, then exploded. Kevin had hit just the right spot. Jagged bloody chunks rained down on the crowd, boinking off shoulders and the bills of hats.

"Wha'd you have to go an' do that for?" Birdseed flicked his cigarette into the dry grass and brushed slabs of meat from his shirt. He advanced on Kevin, taking slow steps. Kevin stepped backward and tripped, falling on his butt.

"Now I know who got ta Adrienne." He spat on Kevin's shirt, then lit another cigarette.

Kennedy burst forward next to Kevin. She wrapped her belt around her knuckles and flicked it toward Birdseed. He laughed so hard his throat seized up, making a tight, wheezy noise. Kevin stood up, pointing the stake in front of him.

"Oh, is that right?" Birdseed said. "Yeh think yeh can take us?" He circled the group as they stood there watching. "Yeh think yeh can take *me*?"

Kevin folded his lips into his mouth and narrowed his eyes. He stood in a boxer's pose, ready to stab whoever got close.

Birdseed narrowed his eyes in return. "Well, seein' as how yer the jackass who killed my girl, I think a lil' balancin' needs to be done here. Don' yeh agree?"

Kennedy gripped her belt tightly. Her head made a small jerk to the side in disagreement. She held her other hand firmly against her back, ready for Birdseed to strike. She wasn't, however, prepared for him to start moving backward. Her gaze followed him as she squeezed the belt tighter than a stress ball.

The sheriff grinned at them, spread out his hands, and presented a slight bow. "How 'bout 'n eye fer an eye?"

The skeletal man moved like a ninja. He sped toward the plinth and leapt onto Brooke's shoulders, ripping out her jugular. Her mouth opened like a fish as a dark red stain swelled over her yellow T-shirt.

"Brooke!" Kevin screamed. Kennedy's ears rang. The crowd became blurry, and she felt woozy.

Brooke dropped her splintered rake; it rattled on the plinth in the dead silence. There were things about Brooke that annoyed Kennedy. There were things she straight-up didn't like about her. She had no plans to stay friends with her back in Springfield, but she didn't deserve that. Kevin didn't deserve that either.

The group descended on her, filling up their cursed jars and licking their fingers as though she were a bucket of fried chicken. Birdseed stood there, folding his arms and smirking at Kevin. His cigarette still poked from his mouth, now covered in Brooke's blood.

He sauntered down the plinth and strolled toward Kevin and Kennedy. Taking the cigarette from his mouth, he pointed at the blood while offering Kevin raised eyebrows, then took an extended drag, locking eyes with him.

"Mmmm," he said. "Best cigarette I e'er had."

"I'll *kill* you, you son of a *bitch*!" Kevin roared, tears running wildly down his face.

"Not if I kill you first." Wyatt snuck up from behind and leapt on Kevin, who spun around, trying to swat at him.

"Check it out, 'seed! I got 'im! Reminds me 'a Big Greasy when he had me!" He chomped down on Kevin, whose eyes turned red and glassy.

Kennedy's heart pounded. It was down to her. She didn't know where Jace was, and her only two friends in this place were hillbilly food. She watched as the undulating throng siphoned the rest of Brooke's blood while Kevin whirled about in front of her in his death throes.

"You must be the leader." Jace marched up from behind Kennedy. The sound of his voice heated up her whole body again. He held the jagged shovel pole; at some point, he had broken it like Brooke had done to the rake.

Birdseed flicked his bloody cigarette and stubbed it out with a heel. Wyatt jumped off Kevin, letting him fall like a brick.

"Nah, not really," Birdseed said. "But, me 'n Wyatt *turned* all these poor folks...if tha's wut ya mean." He stepped toward Jace. "Did'n mean ta, tho'."

"So the *both* of you are the head vampires?" Jace wagged a finger between Birdseed and Wyatt.

Birdseed shrugged. "Sure. If yeh say so."

"So I have to kill both of you to turn these people back to normal?"

Birdseed chuckled. "It don' work like that, son. I *wish* it did. Know why? 'Cuz we'd be okay today too if it did."

Jace stood in front of Kennedy. She took solace in his shadow but poked her head around him to glare at Birdseed.

"How are you even out here?" she hissed.

"Out where, girl? Speak up and make sense." Birdseed nodded toward Kevin, and the hillbilly throng swarmed his body to fill more Mason jars. Kennedy counted five total. She tried to calculate her odds.

"Out *here*," she said. "If you're vampires, how are you out in the sun? You should be dead." She spat out the last word.

Smirking, Birdseed strolled toward her. The familiar smell hit her when he got close enough, and she wrinkled her nose.

"Ain't that what sunscreen's for?" He lit another cigarette and grinned as his lower lip sank under his pointy incisors.

Kennedy's chest heaved as she now realized how she'd been complaining the whole time about the smell, but not knowing it meant she was always so close to a vamp. Close enough to be his or her next animal for slaughter. She thought about the girl in the diner with the blistered skin. She was so young!

Rage rippled in the corners of Kennedy's eyes, coloring her peripheral with red. Her brow prickled with sweat as she knew what she was about to do.

She pushed Jace aside and whipped her belt buckle across Wyatt's face.

"Ow!" he cried, putting a hand to his wound.

She used the distraction to pull out a jagged plank she tore from the shed she held behind her back. She descended on Birdseed and stuck him dead center, just under the ribs. The splintered wood sank easily into his soft, emaciated body.

He coughed and bent over. Kennedy did a squat, then twisted the plank upward, pushing harder into his chest cavity.

"No!" Wyatt screamed and ran to his friend.

Birdseed fell to his knees. He looked up at Wyatt and smiled. "Do yeh think God'll fergive me?"

He exploded.

"No! No! No! Nooooo! James!" Wyatt crawled around in the grass, running his knees through the puddle of Birdseed.

The others stood still, staring at Wyatt and the messy patch of grass.

Wyatt jumped to his feet; dark smears of his friend coated his clothes and face. Veins grew in the whites of his eyes, and he stabbed a finger at Jace. "Eye fer an eye!" he cried.

He bolted toward Jace with the rest of the group. Jace spun around and sprinted toward the fair rides. A couple of the rides were still running with their operators slumped over the controls. A few people were still on the rides, spinning and spinning until they threw up and passed out.

"Go! Get out of here, Kay!" Jace yelled to her as he disappeared into the mix of spinning colors and lights, followed by five vamps.

13

GAMBIT

KENNEDY DIDN'T KNOW WHERE else to go. She'd been in and out of that forest too many times to know it wasn't the place to be.

She stood stiffly in the grass, alone in the center. No hillbillies were nearby, and she had an opportunity that she didn't know what to do with.

Adrienne's sweet tea had destroyed all the cars in the lot. She could run back to Douglas Auto and try to get Jace's car running, but she didn't want to risk a long, treacherous run to find a vehicle that wouldn't move. They had other cars there, but again, there was the dangerous run and the risk of being caught.

She did the only thing she could think of and ran into the demo derby arena.

The remains of the bleachers smoldered, and thick smoke poured from black ashes. Colby's Crusher sat there like a crumpled wad of tin foil, covered in poor Dan Parsons's crusted stain.

But there was the Gambit.

The blue car was pressed against Colby's Crusher but looked relatively unscathed, even from the fire. Kennedy ran to the driver's side, looking every which way for signs of monsters. Did she know how to hotwire a car?

The cracked leather sighed as she slid into the driver's seat. She poked around, looking for ways to start the car while keeping one eye on her surroundings. From the corner of her eye, she saw a twinkle rocking back and forth. The key was in the ignition. Her hand shook as she flipped the key, hearing the glorious growl of an engine turning over. She pumped the gas to hear it again.

She pulled forward, away from the yellow ball of tin foil formerly known as Colby's Crusher. After navigating to the exit of the arena, she was in the open field once again. She ripped through the grass to make a wide loop for the main road.

Just as she was about to turn, Jace stumbled into the field, waving his red shovel handle and limping toward her. She hit the gas and raced toward him, unlocking the door.

"Get in!" she shouted, barely stopping with enough time for Jace to leap into the passenger side.

Jace panted, squeezing the shovel handle until his knuckles went white.

"Did you *kill* them?" she asked.

He nodded, his mouth agape and body tense.

"Jace, are you okay?"

He nodded again, still tense. "Y-yes, I'm fine."

Kennedy dug through the field, throwing clods of sod behind them. Once she hit the main road, the feeling of pavement under the tires had never felt so good.

"Looks like we've got a new car now," she said, chuckling. She tapped the steering wheel.

"Bit of a downgrade." Jace's voice was dry and harsh.

"I'll take it," Kennedy said, punching the gas.

14

BELLY RUB

BEING BACK AT THE apartment made Kennedy feel like she was at the spa. The second the air-conditioned breeze hit her face, she made a beeline for the bathroom.

A quick look in the mirror was enough to show she'd been through hell. The handful of stops they'd made for gas on the way back would have had people talking if she tried to go inside for anything. They both opted to pump and go to avoid stares, no matter how thirsty Jace claimed to be.

Her crusty clothes pooled at her feet, and she stepped into the steaming shower. She sighed, letting the scalding water pummel her skin as she washed the caked-on dirt and the remains of Adrienne from her body. As the whorl of residue circled the drain, she felt a slight twinge of survivor's guilt. She could almost picture the flicker of flames in Brooke's eyes as she stood in stunned surprise just before her demise.

Kevin wasn't terribly strong or brave, and Brooke had her gross habits and annoying frankness, but they had the whole world in front of them. The irony was that they'd actually *chosen* to go to Royal Lake for the fair.

The sheer absurdity of it all turned up the corner of Kennedy's mouth. She shook her head, knowing no one would ever believe their story.

"Hey, Jace!" she shouted from the shower.

He didn't answer. She called out again, but still no answer. She heard faint music playing but couldn't tell what it was. She shrugged, resigned to the fact that he hadn't heard her. She'd talk to him later.

There was merit in at least trying to go to the police and reporting a town full of bloodsucking hillbillies, even if they did laugh her out of the station. She'd go tomorrow. For now, she needed to clean up and take a long nap.

One thing she knew for sure was that she would *never* go to no demo derby ever again.

***

She was right, Jace thought. *I should have taken better care of my car. Now it's gone for good. We missed the concert; Kevin and Brooke are dead, and now I have the worst souvenir from the worst place in the world. I wish I were a better person.*

Jace peered at the bathroom, where Kennedy was showering. He heard the water splashing into the shower pan, no doubt carrying filth with it. He would like to take one after her, but she could take all the time she needs.

He rubbed at his temple, squeezing the pressure point to help stave off the migraine. He felt the blood pump under his skin, its sounds coating his eardrums and drowning out the sound of the shower. His leg ached—a dull ache that felt like poison in his veins.

It was pretty ingenious, really, the way the hillbillies stored the blood they collected. Maybe they didn't really want to kill anyone after all. Does a lion actually *want* to kill the zebra? Or do they just need to feed their pride? Maybe the hillbillies had found clever ways of extending the shelf life, so they only had to kill once a year. At least, that's what he assumed.

Jace strolled over to the radio; the deafening silence was killing him. It was as though he could hear every single blood cell crash against his arteries as they squeezed through his circulatory system. He flipped it on and fidgeted with the tuner until he found soft, crackling guitar tunes. He didn't need hard rock or poppy pop—he just wanted a little soft music to drown out the noises in his head.

While studying the black spider webbing crawling up the length of his leg, he found a small white piece of rock or something still embedded in his ankle. He pulled it out and tossed it on the nightstand to deal with later. A burning dryness scratched his throat, and a searing heat clawed at his eyeballs. His tongue raked the roof of his mouth as though it were sandpaper. He was so very thirsty.

Neither soda, water, or juice felt enough. He needed something thicker and more substantial. Kennedy could help him figure it out.

The sweet crooning of Conway Twitty filled the room, and he thought about his tussle with Wyatt and his friends. It didn't take long to kill them, especially when the other outsiders had regrouped to help. As wiry and clumsy as Wyatt was, he was the hardest to catch. He also went more berserk with every friend who died.

"Tha' wus mah cousin's bes' fren's mama!" Wyatt had cried after Jace had impaled a wild gray-haired woman on the skinny lever of the teacup ride. Fresh tears had run down the previous tear tracks until Wyatt's face was soaking wet and his eyes bloodshot. Jace was surprised to see tears at all.

Taking off the pregnant woman's head with the Tilt-a-Whirl was what drove Jace to vengeance. He told himself that she and her unfortunate child were in a much better place. Especially the baby. What a cruel fate for such an innocent life. All his rage had pulled together in a supersonic nova that had fueled his limbs with the strength and endurance to catch Wyatt.

After getting slammed on the temple by the strongman's mallet Jace had swiped from the comically tall strength-testing game, Wyatt had found himself on the pointy end of Jace's shovel. The vamp had a few moments to grab his ankle, but he wasn't worried because he was confident his makeshift stake had struck true, and it wouldn't be long before Wyatt exploded. Jace thought he heard Wyatt mutter something about vengeance for James, but his head popped midsentence. He must have been hit with some of Wyatt's fleshy pot shot because he felt a sting on his ankle before swiping the shovel handle and sprinting away.

Making it back to the field and spotting Kennedy was like seeing an angel. His ankle hurt, no doubt, but he just had to run to her. He didn't know how to tell her he had to kill so many people to get back to her.

He tried to listen to her shower again, but the rushing blood in his head could only be contained by concentrating on the music. He slipped out of his gore-encrusted shirt and pants and laid a towel on the bed. He then rested on the towel and sank into the pillow to face the ceiling.

Tomorrow, I'd better check and make sure we have enough sunscreen.

He traced his belly button with an index finger, poked it inside, and grinned.

Bonus Short Story

CLIFF CAVE
BOOKS, LLC

The Thief's Folly

The hardest part was dealing with the "skin"—or whatever the outer layer was called. What came underneath, however, was a masterpiece of flavor no being on earth had experienced up to that point—at least, not that I knew of.

I created this one-of-a-kind dish on a hot Thursday in April. We don't get hot days in April here in the North, so this particular day brought with it a certain... anomaly.

I was in my restaurant kitchen as usual, exploring recipes before opening the doors of the ever-popular Vomi Violet. Steam simmered from a pot of rice on the burner while I juggled a series of colored root vegetables-- from my own garden, no less. As I sliced and carved, enjoying the solitude of a patron-less dining area, I heard a little *pink! pink!* come from the pantry.

I knew that sound.

The thief was a slippery little fellow. I supposed he felt the same and thought I would miss him in the act of hauling away an armful of cacao beans from my pantry. I stopped the little Lilliputian in his tracks by hurling my cleaver in his direction. It thunked into the wooden grooves of the floor just in front of his path. My gamble paid off because the absconder froze like a goat.

"What a strange little guy you are," I told him as I bent down for a better look. I don't think he spoke my language, but either way, he would regret treading through my stores. "And what a most vibrant shade of violet." I reached down and touched the velvet fur coating the creature. His beady black eyes glared at me, and another bean went *pink!* to the floor, wobbling away. He sunk his stupid little teeth into the crook of my hand.

"Ow! Damn! You little..." Instinct wrapped my fingers around the handle of the cleaver, and the blade split his skull between those soulless eyes. Oops. The thing teetered and collapsed, spilling the cacao beans everywhere. His body lolled about before coming to a stop.

I sighed and started to pick up the beans when my nose caught the most decadent aroma. Purple ooze dribbled like honey from the creature's head wound, creating a glimmering pool underneath him. I wiggled my nostrils to pull in more of the scent, and I struck a wild plan.

After fighting with the removal of the skin to reveal the ooey gooey goodness of the center, I wondered whether I should attempt to make a nice jerky from the velveteen flesh. No one ever sampled purple jerky before. Well... not that I knew of.

In the meantime, I crafted one of the most beautiful and intricate appetizers in my career. The consistency of the little guy's innards was perfect for spherification. I created several plates of violet "faux roe" with a side of an orange balsamic reduction.

I put the last touches on the final plate when the first of many patrons scuttled into my restaurant, practically demanding the apéritif du jour the second their foot hit the threshold. *What would I call the lovely pile of purple popping boba?*

I wanted so eagerly to introduce this experimental appetizer to the crowd. After years of enduring their snobbish reviews and countless critiques, they would truly get something worth talking about. Who had any inkling what the effects of intergalactic guts on an earthy digestive tract could be?

After a myriad of plates were delivered and the familiar sounds of clinking forks hitting the ceramic and sliding between polished veneers rang through the room, I began my rounds, stopping at the nearest table where a slender nerd and his woman sat.

"Excuse me, what did you say this was called again?" the nerd asked. He perched his nose so far up in the air I could slide quarters into his nostrils before he realized it. The woman across from him blinked and extended her lips into a crumpled pursing.

"The Thief's Folly," I answered, grinning at the pair. They took tiny bites, sliding their tongues around in their disgusting mouths, then nodded in approval and shooed me away. "Please enjoy." I turned back to the counter to observe the dining area.

Several murmurs rose through the crowd. Declarations of "the finest dish ever sold" to "like nothing I've ever tasted!" were common utterances among the elite. Of course, they were correct— the aroma I experienced told me it would be amazing in the mouth... but how would it settle? The sting of anticipation gnawed at me as the patrons reveled in the spoonfuls of the galaxy.

Then, the groaning began.

The pursed-lip woman across from the nerd spewed a wave of violet so explosive in his face it blew off his spectacles. He returned the favor. Patrons slid from their seats, attempting to make a dash for the toilet but failing and making more of a mess of things.

The dining room filled with a cacophony of wails and guttural stomach noises. A splatter here, a mudslide there... some of them slipped around and fell in the muck, rolling through and adding to it. I was sure I saw a whole boiled egg come out of someone, along with pieces of my thieving friend.

Shoes squeaked on the polished floor as guests scrambled here and there, drowning out my fine French orchestral music. Pleas to make it stop threaded through the din with a tiny tinkle of laughter—and it wasn't me!

I crossed my arms and smiled at the chaos.

Wonder no longer, this was what happened when one ate extraterrestrial insides... Maybe I would try to make that jerky after all.

About the Author

 R.E. HOLDING WAS BORN in 1979 in Iowa and lives in Missouri with her husband and four cats. She studied educational science and pharmacology and works as a scientific project manager. While not typing away at the keyboard, she is working full-time, reading, watching movies, cooking, or making soap (www.lhsoaps.com). Her favorite genres are horror, sci-fi, and fantasy—and in 2023, she founded Cliff Cave Books, LLC, dedicated to creating stories in those genres.

www.cliffcavebooks.com

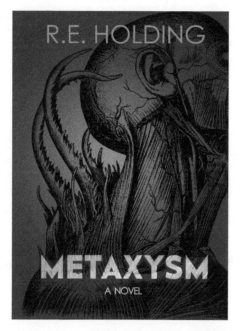

METAXYSM: A Creature Feature Horror
https://mybook.to/lLdVpm

Don't forget— if you enjoyed HILLBILLY VAMP, why not write a review? I would love to hear what you think!

VISIT THE BLOG AT

 www.cliffcavebooks.com

FEATURES OF THE SITE:

- Updates &Reviews
- Upcoming Works
- Author Site
- Online Store
- Special Requests

Join the email list to receive blog updates, special offers, reviews, giveaways, and more. Stay in touch!

Milton Keynes UK
Ingram Content Group UK Ltd.
UKHW011144100424
440866UK00004B/189